THE S

MICH

When Ginny Luellen, the horse-mad Horse goes to Ireland with her mother, she is hoping to have an unforgettable holiday. But she doesn't expect, on the first day, to find a dappled grey thoroughbred tethered in the middle of a stream. Despite her mother's advice not to interfere, Ginny is determined to find out what is going on and tracks down not only the horse's owner, but also another identical grey. Which horse is being ridden in the local races, and can Ginny make sure both are safe?

For Karl

Best wich

Michael Hardcastle

in

Whitley

1994

MICHAEL HARDCASTLE

The Switch Horse

MAMMOTH

First published in Great Britain 1980
by Methuen Children's Books Ltd
Magnet paperback edition published 1982

Published 1990 by Mammoth
an imprint of Mandarin Paperbacks
Michelin House, 81 Fulham Road, London SW3 6RB

Mandarin is an imprint of the Octopus Publishing Group

Text copyright © 1979 Michael Hardcastle
Illustrations copyright © 1979 Methuen Children's Books Ltd

ISBN 0 7497 0442 X

A CIP catalogue record for this title
is available from the British Library

Printed in Great Britain
by Cox and Wyman Ltd, Reading, Berkshire

One

The producer was plainly exasperated. It was bad enough that his leading lady was, so she said, suffering an attack of migraine; and that her stand-in had no understanding at all of the role she was supposed to be playing. To make matters worse, the entire cast appeared to have lost its collective sense of timing.

'What are you *doing* to me?' he appealed to them, his hands clasping his chest as if to demonstrate just where the pain was most affecting him. 'This is supposed to be a comedy and *this* is supposed to be one of the funny bits, the *really* funny bits. So timing is everything. If your response, Maggy, is delayed by more than a split-second the laugh is lost – the whole point of the scene is lost.' Ralph Bigley paused and then murmured: 'And so are we.

Might as well never have come here if we can't do better than this.'

That final remark was audible to everyone, as it was meant to be. Ralph had been an actor himself in his younger days and he knew perfectly well how to command attention by lowering his voice at a critical moment.

'But, Ralph darling, I can't make my response if the cue is wrong, now can I?' Maggy asked in the sweetest tone. Then she turned to Vicki and the smile she gave her was quite dazzling. 'Sorry, Vicki darling, but you did get your line wrong, you know. I was waiting for you to correct it, you see.'

Vicki, stand-in for the leading lady, nodded. 'Sorry, Maggy. But I wasn't sure whether – '

Ralph cut in promptly to regain control of the rehearsal. 'One wrong word at this stage doesn't matter that much. You ought to know that, Maggy. The *vital* thing is to get the whole play flowing – everything running like a well-tuned engine, no hiccups, no stutterings.'

In the fourth row of the stalls Bill Anderson leaned towards the slim, chestnut-haired girl sitting beside him and remarked: 'I think old Ralph up there would be much happier in a garage. Sounds more like an engineer than a producer of plays. All that tuning-up stuff and so on. Actors

8

and actresses are people, not engine components. Don't you agree, Ginny?'

Ginny Luellen just nodded, though with as much enthusiasm as she could muster. She was rather enjoying the experience of attending a play rehearsal, all the more so because her mother was a member of the cast. She felt she would have enjoyed it still more had she been on her own for Mr Anderson's frequent comments were simply ruining her concentration. Unfortunately, he had no one else to talk to for he and Ginny comprised the entire audience. It was his wife, Nancy, who was the missing leading lady.

The play was a comedy-thriller called *Don't look at me like that!* and the company presenting it was the Corwick Amateur Dramatic Society. Corwick was the Cotswold village where all the players lived and they put on a couple of plays a year, mainly for their own pleasure, in the Community Centre. A few months earlier the Society, to the astonishment of most of the members, had received an invitation to take part in an Amateur Drama Festival in Ireland.

For Ginny it was a stroke of luck that the Festival was to take place in the week that was her half-term holiday. Her mother had suggested that Ginny should go with them to Ireland. 'It'll be good for you to have a change of scenery, Ginny, and I'll be glad to have some family support,' was how Mrs Luellen had put it. Some of the cast were taking their husbands or wives with them and treating the trip as an extra holiday.

Ginny's father, a sales representative, was much too busy with a seasonal marketing campaign to spare the time to accompany his wife to Ireland. 'I expect he won't even notice that we've gone,' Jane Luellen remarked. Ginny was inclined to agree. Even when he was at home her father seemed always to have masses of returns to fill in and complicated mathematical calculations to make. At regular intervals he faithfully promised to do something about sharing in Ginny's devotion to horses, but somehow he never got round to it. Ginny didn't really mind that: usually she was perfectly happy to pursue her interests on her own.

The visit to the Festival was her first trip abroad: though, it had to be admitted, the west coast of Ireland scarcely seemed like a foreign land. After all, everyone spoke English, even if the accent was very different from the ones she heard at home. To her the greatest joy of the holiday was that Ireland was the land of the horse. Many of the greatest race-horses she'd heard about, including the legendary triple Grand National winner, Red Rum, had been born here. So she was looking forward to exploring the countryside around the small town of Ballytor where they were staying. With luck, she might even come across a small racing stable similar to the one run by Richard McDade near her home in Corwick. Mr McDade and his wife, Janet, had befriended Ginny and she spent most of her free time helping to look after one of their horses, Tamela, nowadays the undoubted star of the Plumtree Lane Stables.

The Corwick ADS had arrived in Ballytor the previous evening and so today was being spent in rehearsals. Eager as she was to go off on her own, Ginny had felt it was only fair to her mother to show some interest in their play. As she'd become well aware from the various discussions on the journey from England, it wasn't everyone's choice. Some members of the cast seemed quite horrified by the idea of presenting a comedy-thriller as their entry. They were of the opinion that a play with a 'message', or at least something of a more serious nature, would have given them a better chance of success.

Ginny gathered that Nancy Anderson, the leading lady, was among those who held that view. Jane Luellen had hinted to her daughter, as they arrived at the hall being used for the rehearsal, that Mrs Anderson's migraine attack was no more than a means of demonstrating her disapproval to Ralph Bigley. For it was he who had made the final decision about the choice of play. He had argued that the Society should 'do something different – and you can't do better than amuse your audience *and* thrill them at the same time.' It wasn't easy for anyone to deny the truth of that statement.

Don't look at me like that! was about the mysterious death of an undertaker. It might have been murder and, again, it might not. Whichever it was, a lot of people who knew him had a lot of explaining to do. His new widow, on whom plenty of suspicion was to fall, was being played by Maggy Newsome. But even her role was not as important as that of the late undertaker's lady partner, the part that had been awarded to Nancy Anderson.

Jane Luellen had yet to make her entrance, but she was waiting in the wings. Her role, too, was that of a widow – but a young and rich widow – and she joked to Ginny when landing in Ireland: 'I rather feel like a widow, though hardly a rich one. Do you know, this is the first time I've ever been away without your Dad since we married. And that was fifteen years ago.'

'Never mind, Mum, we'll send him heaps of postcards so he'll know we're thinking about him – and missing him,' Ginny had replied sympathetically. She had a long list of other people she was going to bombard with postcards. It would be fun dreaming up appropriate messages and fitting the cards to them. So far there hadn't been an opportunity to look round the shops for postcards or anything else but, apart from Mr Anderson, no one would miss her when she decided she'd had enough of the rehearsal. Watching people she knew pretending to be someone else was often amusing, but the constant repetition of various exhanges of dialogue was becoming a bore.

Ginny made her way slowly to the back of the hall and then paused, hoping to catch her mother's eye and signal that she was leaving. But, like every other member of the cast, Mrs Luellen was giving her undivided attention to the producer. With Ralph in such an explosive mood anything might happen at any moment. Jane Luellen had no intention of becoming his next victim, especially as she was just about to make her entrance.

Rather to Ginny's surprise, Ballytor was bathed in sunshine. In the fairly gloomy hall she hadn't been aware of the weather and so she'd assumed that the light rain falling at breakfast-time was still falling. Everyone had warned her before leaving home that it rained perpetually in Ireland: that was why the grass was so green and the country was called the Emerald Isle. Well, it was nice to know that all the experts were wrong about one thing at least.

Momentarily, she was undecided what to do.

Her intention had been to look round the town (something that probably wouldn't take long, anyway), write a few postcards and then return to the rehearsal and join the cast for their lunch break. But the sight of such lovely sunshine had given her a fresh idea. It was a perfect day for a picnic: beside the sea, perhaps, or right out in the country where she might encounter some horses.

She mentally ticked off the list of things she would need as she strolled down the main street which, fittingly and simply, was called Main Street. So far as she could see there was no official bus stop and nowhere any sign of a timetable that would suggest a likely destination, for she was quite prepared to choose her spot on the basis of an attractive name. She supposed that there *were* buses, since there certainly weren't any trains, but perhaps they were infrequent: which was how it was at home. Now, if only there was a horse for hire ...! That would solve her transport problem beautifully, especially as she was rich enough at the moment to pay for a ride. Since hearing about the trip to the Festival she had saved frantically. The money that Mr McDade insisted on paying her for helping to look after Tamela had mounted impressively. So it was going to be a holiday to remember for ever.

An enticing display of chocolates drew her to the window of what she imagined would be described

as a general store, rather like the Post Office in Corwick. It had to be general because, incongruously,
the chocolates were surrounded by items of fishing
tackle, boxes of biscuits, jars of honey and wooden
bowls of dried fruits. Perhaps, she reflected with

amusement, fishermen in Ireland needed plenty to sustain them if there were long intervals between catching fish.

Within the store the route to the counter was almost an obstacle course. She had to pick her way with care between small mountains of cartons, coils of rope, fishermen's nets spread wide from hooks on beams, crates of vegetables and a rack of knobbly-topped walking sticks. In all, it was a remarkable collection of merchandise and Ginny wished she'd had a friend with her to exclaim over it.

'Well, now, and what is it I'll be getting for you?' a voice asked. Ginny had thought the shop was empty, but now she spotted someone at the far end of the counter, half-hidden by a curtain made of strings of beads. Then the shopkeeper stepped forward and Ginny saw that he was quite a young man with such a mass of curly black hair that he appeared to have a halo. Yet the style of the shop had suggested that it would be run by an ancient and forgetful eccentric.

'Oh, good morning,' said Ginny brightly. 'I'd like some chocolate, some apples – two big juicy ones, please – a bag of crisps, those with a cheesy flavour – and do you have an orange drink, but not the fizzy sort?'

The man was nodding pleasantly. 'Sure now, I

think we can manage that little list. I'm thinking it's a picnic you've set your heart on, now isn't that so?'

Ginny grinned. 'Absolutely right. Actually, I was going to ask you about buses. I haven't seen one in Ballytor yet and I want to go out into the country.'

'Well now, the buses are not running very well from here, you see. People here are not big travellers – they like to stay at home.' As he spoke he was weighing apples on one of the most modern machines she'd ever seen: so up to date that it had a built-in price calculator. 'But you needn't be bothering your head about buses. There's a bicycle here that you can be using with the greatest of pleasure.'

'A bike! Oh yes, that would be lovely – just the day for it.' Ginny was thinking that, indeed, a bike was the next best thing to a horse for such a trip. 'You mean you'd hire it to me?'

'Not at all, no, no. You just take the loan of it with the compliments of McCormick's. It's very welcome to it you are.'

Ginny was overwhelmed by such unexpected generosity. Why, the man had no idea who she was, no idea whether she could be trusted to –

'You're on holiday now, aren't you? And to be sure you'll be wanting to enjoy yourself,' he was continuing as if reading her mind. 'We'll be seeing plenty of you, I trust, and you'll be telling all your friends, the theatrical people I'm thinking, that McCormick's can supply all their shopping needs – and at the most competitive prices you could be finding in all Ireland. Now, that's the truth I'm telling you.'

Ginny had to laugh. 'I see! So I'm going to be your mobile advertisement, is that it?'

His grin was as mischievous as it was friendly. 'You could be saying that!' he agreed.

Next moment he'd disappeared through the bead curtain and when he returned he was wheeling a silver-and-blue cycle.

'Oh, terrific,' Ginny exclaimed. 'And it's even got a saddle-bag for my picnic goodies! Perfect.'

She paid for the goodies but barely listened to Mr McCormick's recommendations in regard to routes she might take to find the best picnic spots. She wanted to discover them for herself. But she remembered to thank the storekeeper again for his kindness and promise to return the bike that evening.

'You'll be after keeping it the whole week, I'm thinking, so don't you be worrying about that,' he assured her.

He came to the door to give her a farewell wave and Ginny thought that was a lovely gesture. She wondered, as she pedalled away, whether all the Irish people she was going to meet on her travels would be so kind-hearted to a complete stranger.

Two

The town was soon behind her. Houses on both sides of the narrow, metalled road had given way to low, stone walls and hedges and the countryside was all around her. Ginny had no idea where she was heading, except that she thought it was in the general direction of the coast, but that didn't matter: it made it more of an adventure. Across neatly divided fields she could make out farm buildings and, at intervals, quite solitary bungalows that looked to be very modern in style and construction. But of people there was no sign at all.

After a few miles she at last arrived at crossroads just when she was beginning to think that she really was on the longest road of all because it had no turning. The directions that she could choose from, however, were far less interesting than the pair of donkeys grazing at the foot of the signpost. A mare

20

and her foal, their colouring was a rich, dark brown; they stopped feeding to give Ginny a speculative look that seemed to indicate that they imagined she had brought something for them.

'Oh, you're gorgeous – yes, both of you,' she greeted them, coming to a halt beside them by putting one foot on the ground. Immediately the mare came forward, nudging Ginny forcefully in the region of the ribs and almost causing her to topple over. 'Hey, be careful!' Ginny responded warningly. 'Don't damage the bike. It isn't mine, you know. You ought to be able to tell that because it's Irish, and so are you!'

A feeble joke was not what the mare wanted: a titbit was. Already her teeth were dragging at Ginny's pocket and, when they found nothing appetising there, they switched to an attack on the saddle-bag.

'Lay off!' Ginny said, pushing the mare's nose away. 'That's my lunch, the only one I've got. Look, have a mint – if Tamela adores them I'm sure you will.'

By now the foal was thrusting into her midriff in search of his share and between them the donkeys consumed the entire packet of mints in a couple of minutes with much satisfying scrunching. Ginny decided she'd better make a quick getaway before they could hijack the apples. She herself was

beginning to feel hungry, but this was hardly the place to have a peaceful picnic.

Swinging herself back on to the bike, she instinctively took the road to the left. She hadn't taken note of any of the names on the signpost, but one road was as good as another in her present mood. When she risked a glance over her shoulder she saw that the donkeys were following her: they weren't exactly galloping, but they still had an air of determination about them. Doubtless they were working on the principle that their benefactress must stop again sooner or later and so they'd catch up with her and get another tasty snack.

'No chance,' Ginny sung out to her pursuers. 'One of my apples is for the first *horse* I meet who deserves it. You donkeys have had all you're getting.'

As she rode along she wondered about the donkeys' owner, always supposing they had one. Had they got loose from his field or did they run wild, roaming at will rather like the ponies on Dartmoor and in the New Forest? True enough, they did look rather unkempt, though that was not unusual in donkeys. Next time she looked round there was no sign of mare or foal so it seemed they had given up the chase. Doubtless they would make the most of the next encounter with another passer-by. So far, though, the roads Ginny had travelled had been quite deserted; she was beginning to get the feeling that she was the only human being on the move in the whole of Ireland.

Soon the road to wherever it was began to dip and pass between high banks topped by hedges and clumps of trees. No sooner had she started to free-wheel than the highway became a switch-back and she had to pedal hard to cope with the gradient. It was then that the first car she'd seen since setting out came shooting past her in the opposite direction; because it was straddling the white line it was a close enough shave for her to be thankful that there weren't more drivers about to threaten her progress.

By the time she reached the summit of the ascent she decided she'd had quite enough cycling for one morning. Even on such a light and sweetly moving machine it was a far more exhausting business than riding a horse, even a hard-puller. The landscape, she saw, had opened out again into what looked like a vast expanse of moorland dotted with boulders and huge slabs of rock. However, when she dismounted she found that the trampoline-like turf wasn't quite so flat as she'd supposed: in the middle distance and beyond it fell away into gullies and saucer-shaped hollows.

Ginny pushed the bike towards the nearest outcrop of rock near the rim of one of the hollows. It was a good spot to have her meal: she could rest her back against the stone, enjoy a view that seemed

25

to stretch for miles and feel that she had the whole world to herself, not just the Emerald Isle. Her horizons, she decided as she munched her way through a bar of chocolate, were definitely expanding. It was a pity she hadn't brought a book because a long, uninterrupted read would have been guaranteed; in the flurry of surprise surrounding Mr McCormick's offer to lend her the cycle she had also forgotten to buy any postcards so she couldn't pass the time by writing those, either. Only one thing to do: have a nap. The exertion of pedalling, the food and the warmth of the sun had combined to make her drowsy, anyway.

She lay down and started to think about the Drama Festival and the rehearsal she'd watched: it was funny the way they all took it so seriously, especially as it was supposed to be a comedy – well, more of a comedy than a thriller, so far as she could judge. Even her mother, normally a fairly relaxed person, became really tense when she knew she was going to have to perform on stage. At breakfast that morning she'd hardly listened to anything Ginny said and then, when the comments had been repeated with very careful enunciation, shown unusual signs of irritation.

'You know, Mum, I honestly think you're all dead scared of your Mr Bigley,' Ginny remarked with mock-seriousness.

'Nonsense!' Jane Luellen retaliated spiritedly. 'He *is* the producer and this Festival is very important to him. He is depending on every one of us to do our best and we mustn't let him down. If you're going to take that attitude, Ginny, I may begin to wish that you'd stayed at home to look after your father.'

Ginny's thoughts drifted back to Corwick. Inevitably, they centred on Plumtree Lane Stables and, in particular, on Tamela, the chestnut hurdler ('pale as gold' was how she described his colouring) who filled her life with so much happiness. Perhaps he, too, was having a snooze, or pretending to, after his morning's exercise gallops. He'd then be looking forward to his evening feed and the cosseting he would get now, in Ginny's absence, from Janet McDade.

'Oh, this is ridiculous!' Ginny said aloud, jumping to her feet. 'I'm not really tired at all and I don't want to go to sleep. Only old people have a nap in the afternoon. Exercise is what *I* need, on foot, not on two wheels.'

At that moment she heard a familiar noise: the neighing of a horse. Momentarily, the coincidence was so startling that she couldn't believe that's what it was. Just when her mind had been concentrated on Tamela....

Then it came again: obviously from some distance but still distinctive. There could be no mistaking that sound in Ginny's ears. There was no other in the world like it.

Without a thought for the bike she had propped against the other side of the boulder, she raced off in the direction from which the sounds seemed to come. The springy turf might have been made for a runner and Ginny bounded over it in great strides.

Soon the ground ahead of her began to slope downwards, gently at first, then with increasing steepness. Ginny found herself on the edge of what looked like a miniature ravine. She could hear the noise of tumbling water some distance below the point where she stood. Suddenly it occurred to her that perhaps the horse had made its way down to the watercourse to drink and was trapped.

She began to scramble down the banking, grabbing for support at vegetation and the occasional exposed root of small bushes. Still there was no sign of the horse and no further sound from it. Had she, after all, simply imagined it? No, definitely not: the noise had been real enough. One other possibility came to mind: that the animal, quietly grazing, had been startled by something, had naturally expressed its alarm or displeasure vocally, and then galloped off. On such terrain its hooves, of course, would have made no sound audible over any distance at all.

'Well, just as long as you're safe and well nothing else matters,' Ginny told the invisible horse. 'But I do want to *see* that you're all right.'

At last she caught sight of the stream: narrow and flowing with considerable force over a series of rocky ledges that rather resembled the steps of an escalator. It was also beautifully clear. Ginny slithered down to the edge of the stream and scooped some water up with both hands to splash it over her face. Until that moment, she hadn't realized how hot she was.

Just below the point where Ginny stood, the stream swirled away to the right past a bank with an almost vertical face. If the horse was still in the vicinity then he had to be somewhere down there. Gingerly, she made her way along the bank, now and again clutching at tough little bushes to save herself from slipping into the water. She hadn't paused to roll up the legs of her jeans and now her foothold was too precarious to allow that operation.

She reached the bend in the stream. And it was from there that she saw the horse, a dappled grey.

'Oh, my goodness, what on earth are you doing there?' Ginny exclaimed. 'Oh, you poor, poor thing!'

For the grey was standing, quite motionless and facing towards her, in the very centre of the stream.

The water was foaming round him, just above the height of his knees, and when he spotted Ginny his ears pricked up and he wickered softly. Yet still he made no attempt to move so much as an inch.

Ginny, thoroughly shaken, couldn't immediately understand why he should remain so still. Then, as she took a step forward, it became quite obvious. The horse was hobbled, though in an extraordinary manner. A line stretched out to him from either bank: one was fastened below the knee of his near foreleg, the other to his off hindleg.

The young grey was as securely moored in the middle of the stream as any small boat might have been.

Three

Without pausing to think about any risk, Ginny plunged into the stream. Her one aim was to free the horse and lead him out of the water. Even though the sun was warm the water was not: it was distinctly chilly and, if he'd been standing in it for some time, he must by now be suffering severely from exposure. The grey showed only momentary alarm at her rapid approach: he laid back his ears but, as soon as Ginny started to talk softly to him, they flicked forward again.

She ran her hand down his leg, seeking the place where the line was fastened. It was only when her fingers located it, well below the level of the water, that she realized how stupid she'd been. For, of course, the lines would run from the banks, round the legs and back again. She hadn't even checked to see how they were secured. Immersion in the stream had tautened the lines, which seemed to be made of a kind of twine, and three-ply twine at that. Ginny had no illusions about how tough it was going to be to break. But then, naturally, it would have to be very strong indeed to restrain a horse.

Her only hope was to cut it with something: but with what? She wasn't carrying a knife or any implement that would serve as a substitute. Unless she could find a stone with a really sharp edge. . . .

'Don't worry, grey horse, I'm not deserting you,' Ginny assured him as she scrambled up onto the bank again. Her search, however, was fruitless. Every stone she picked up was smooth with rounded corners as if they had all been constantly washed by the stream when it was in spate. So she turned her attention to the place where the line was secured.

Her heart sank again when she saw that the cord was held down by an iron stake driven deeply into the ground. There was no hope at all of removing it with her bare hands. Clearly it had been fixed by someone who knew exactly what he was doing so that even a determined horse couldn't pull itself free.

Ginny's sense of utter frustration was making her furious with herself. But she remembered not to let the horse become aware of her mood. As it was, he remained remarkably calm.

'You must have a wonderful temperament,'

33

Ginny said, wading out to him again. 'I can't think many horses would stand for the treatment someone's been dishing out to you. But, whoever it is, I'll find him. Listen, grey horse: I'll be back as soon as I can. I'm off to get help. And I'll bring something back that you'll really like, something to help make up for what you've suffered.'

The horse merely eyed her retreat with interest as she climbed out of the stream. Not once had he flinched when she touched him. He's a stoic, that's what he is, a stoic, Ginny told herself. Already she was beginning to think that her next task would be to find a good home for him. First, though, he had to be freed from the water torture.

She had started to make her way down-stream, believing that it would lead her to a town or village where probably the horse's owner lived. Then it occurred to her that it might be miles away: better, therefore, to collect the bike and cycle there. As she pulled herself up the steepest part of the bank and regained the moorland she rehearsed the scorching comments she would make when she found and tackled the sadist in question.

It didn't take her long to reach the place where she'd left the bike. 'And to think,' she told herself, 'that less than an hour ago I was just lying here, enjoying a picnic, while Grey Horse was suffering like that.'

The moorland was quickly behind and above her as the road began to descend in a series of gentle, swinging curves. Under other circumstances she would have enjoyed that ride. Trees and hedgerows reappeared and she could sense that the sea was not very far away – the sea into which that stream would flow. At the sight of the first cottage she slowed, thinking that perhaps she should make an inquiry there. But it was tiny, with a shut-up look about it; and, anyway, Ginny knew that country people could be very wary about talking to strangers, especially about themselves and the place where they lived. It would be best to go straight into the town.

Skelhouley said the signpost at the foot of the last hill: Skelhouley, 1 mile. Not for the first time Ginny marvelled at the originality of Irish place-names. Although she hadn't really known what to expect, the town, when she reached it, was a disappointment. A single street, dog-legged but unexpectedly wide, lined with cold grey cottages, some dreadfully pebble-dashed and showing cracks like fissures, a couple of bars and as many shops, not a splash of real colour to be seen anywhere.

She stopped outside one of the shops, which appeared to sell hardware among its oddments, and marched in. Predictably, it was thoroughly gloomy and there was no one to be seen. With a coin she rapped on the counter: this was no time for waiting patiently. The shopkeeper, when he came, was, predictably also, not another Mr McCormick: old-ish, unshaven in a grubby open-necked shirt and trousers tied with rough string. No welcome, no smile, no word of any kind.

'I'd like a knife, please, with a very sharp blade – sharp enough to cut cord that's very strong.'

He moved away, still silent, and rummaged in a drawer. When he found something she wouldn't have been surprised if he'd slapped it down on the counter with a take-it-or-leave-it attitude.

Instead, he laid it in front of her very tenderly as if it were a choice gift; in fact, it was a fearsome weapon with a black, studded handle and a wicked-looking point.

''Tis a lot of damage you could be doing with that,' said the shopkeeper in a soft but suspicious voice. Ginny wasn't going to argue. The price was very reasonable (well, at least tourists aren't over-charged here, she decided) and when she paid for it the man slipped the money straight into his pocket.

She hesitated and then asked: 'Do you know anyone here who has a grey horse? Dappled grey – about three or four, I should think – and a thoroughbred.'

36

There was no immediate response. It was as if the man was debating whether to answer at all. His gaze was over her shoulder and Ginny found the temptation to look round almost irresistible. Surely though, it was an innocent enough question: so what was preventing him from giving her a straight answer?

Eventually, and as softly as before: 'Lot of horses around here, there are. Lot of them are grey. Some chestnut, some brown, one or two mixtures, ye might say. More greys than anything. Ye can't be telling them apart, often enough.'

'Yes, but –' Ginny started to say. Then, realizing that his deviousness was deliberately designed to defeat her inquiry, she decided there was no point in pursuing it. 'Oh, never mind. It's not important. Good-bye.'

She was confident he wouldn't utter another word as she walked out of the shop, and she was right. She put the knife in her saddle-bag and glanced along the street. Only one person was in sight: an elderly man walking with the obviously necessary aid of a stick. Had she been at home in the Cotswolds he was just the sort of man who would know everybody and everything that was going on and be happy to tell her what *she* wanted to know. Here in Skelhouley, she feared, he'd be another barrier of silence faced by a stranger.

37

Although she now had the means to free the grey horse from his bonds, it occurred to her that it might be a good idea to see what else there was in the village. It would take no more than a couple of minutes to cycle from one end to the other: and that way she just might spot some stables or evidence of other places where horses were kept. She had heard stories that in Ireland horses had been kept in byres with the cows, in tin sheds at the bottom of gardens, in muddy lean-to's at the end of nowhere. Such horses were sometimes thoroughbreds, or highly promising steeple-chasers, which the owners didn't want the racing world to hear too much about; thus, when they raced they were almost literally 'dark horses' and might win at a nice price and benefit only their owners and trainers.

At a very casual pace Ginny rode down the street, hoping that it might appear that she was just taking a gentle spin and showing no interest in anything in particular. She couldn't avoid the feeling that she was most probably under observation from this cottage or that, but if that was so then the watchers were taking good care not to show themselves. Overtaking the man with the walking stick, she called a cheery 'Good afternoon'; he waved his free hand in a semi-greeting and that was more encouraging.

38

Ginny was just on the point of turning back, and then pedalling like mad to return to Grey Horse, when she passed the narrow entrance to an alleyway. It was between a cottage and what looked like an empty shop and she thought she could detect, right at the far end, a stable yard. She hopped off the bike, propped it against the side wall of the shop and set off to investigate on foot. Already she'd decided that if anyone challenged her she'd simply reply that she was 'exploring'. They could make what they liked of that.

Nonetheless, she made her way down the passage in some trepidation: she had no idea what or who she might encounter and she couldn't help wondering whether she would recognize the 'sadist' if she came face to face with him. But there was no one about and the yard into which the alleyway led was a disappointment. All it contained was junk of various kinds: large chunks of rusting metal, broken machinery, a huge wheel without a tyre and a pile of wooden crates. There were a couple of stone outbuildings on the far side of the yard, but apart from some smelly sacks and a scattering of feathers they held nothing of interest. Not a hint of a horse anywhere.

She'd been wasting her time. She turned to leave – and then stopped dead. For someone was now standing at the end of the passageway, just inside

39

the yard, and watching her intently: a small, thin
girl in a blue-and-white floral patterned dress that
was very short indeed.

'Oh, hello,' said Ginny, recovering quickly. 'I
didn't hear you arrive.'

The girl looked down at her feet as if that remark
needed an explanation. And indeed she had the sort
of footwear that would make no sound at all: plim-

solls. Her ankle socks were scarcely any whiter than her shoes. Ginny guessed that the girl was about a couple of years younger than herself, say about eleven, and she gave the impression she was shy.

'Hi, I'm Ginny Luellen. What's your name?'

'Carmen.' The voice was stronger than Ginny had imagined it would be: but very musically Irish in intonation. Carmen was now looking at her with a very steady gaze.

'Do you live near here, Carmen?'

'Just along the street, not far. What are you doing in here? This is Mr Gilligan's yard.'

'Ah. He doesn't keep horses, does he?'

'He doesn't keep anything. He hasn't any work now.'

Ginny wasn't sure whether that was meant to be a joke or not. Carmen gave the information very matter-of-factly but that could be her style of humour, Ginny supposed. Still, the girl was more forthcoming than the shopkeeper had been. Ginny was beginning to feel just a little better about what went on in Skelhouley.

'The point is, Carmen, I'm interested in a horse, a dappled grey. A thoroughbred, I think. A really lovely horse, aged about three or four.'

'Is it your own horse then?'

'Oh no, of course not! I'm just a visitor here. I live in England, you see. No, I saw this horse in a – well, up on the moors. And I wondered who owned him. Does anybody in the village have a grey horse?'

As soon as she'd asked that question she remembered what the shopkeeper had told her. If Carmen confirmed that the place was full of greys, well, Ginny might as well give up her attempt to identify the one in the stream just by asking questions of anybody she met.

'Well, I have seen a grey horse in our town,' Carmen replied cautiously. Then, in a rush: 'But I don't know who his owner is. I wouldn't be wanting to say anything about that – not to, well, not to someone from over the water.'

That phrase mystified Ginny. 'From *over the water*?'

Carmen looked a trifle embarrassed. 'From England. That's what we say about people who live there, over the Irish Sea.'

'Oh yes, I get it. *Of course*. But why is it all a secret – about the grey horse, I mean?'

Half-turning away, Carmen appeared to be concentrating on straightening the hem of her dress. Ginny recognized that sign of embarrassment only too well. But what was so embarrassing about her questions?

'Carmen, what is it? What's worrying you? Look, I'm only trying to help.' She paused, then added on inspiration: 'I promise I wouldn't tell anybody you'd told me if that's what you want. Nobody would have a clue where I'd got my information from.'

With obvious reluctance, Carmen turned to face her again. 'Ah, but they would, y'see,' she answered in that soft lilting tone. 'Here, everyone knows everything about everybody. 'Tis just a tiny place, Skelhouley is. So I'm not after saying a word about Mr Caff – I mean, about the racehorse.'

Ginny's eyes widened in relief and delight. 'Oh, so he *is* a racehorse! I thought he might be. You see, I work with a racehorse in Corwick, where I live. A beautiful chestnut called Tamela. You'd adore him, too, Carmen. Oh, look – '

But Carmen now knew she'd said too much. The word 'racehorse' had been a fatal one to use. 'Look, I've got to be going, right now. I've things to do that can't wait. I would have liked to talk to you properly – about England and suchlike things. Maybe . . .'

Then, even before the last word was out of her mouth, she was running – running as hard as she could down the passageway to the street. Carmen's speed astonished Ginny almost as much as the manner of her departure.

Ginny followed her at walking pace. Then she, too, began to hurry. She had neglected the grey horse long enough; now she wished that she had gone to free him the moment she'd acquired the knife. When she reached the street there was no sign of Carmen; thankfully, the cycle was just where she'd left it.

All kinds of thoughts were whirling round her head as fast as the wheels as she raced out of Skelhouley and headed for the moor. She couldn't begin to imagine why her questions had so alarmed Carmen that the girl had simply run away. But that Carmen knew a great deal about the horse – and, most important, who owned him – was not in doubt.

Ginny couldn't concentrate her mind on that mystery now as she struggled up the hill. When she reached the summit and turned off the road on to the moorland she paused for only a moment to get her breath back before bouncing across the turf to the bank of the stream. Grabbing the knife from her saddle-bag, she scrambled down to the water and made her way to the bend in the stream.

'I'm here, Grey Horse, I'm here!' she yelled to alert him to her return. But this time she heard no whinny of welcome. A moment later she saw why there was no greeting.

The grey horse had vanished.

Four

'Ginny, it's absolutely none of your business,' said Jane Luellen in her so-let's-have-no-more-of-that voice.

In spite of that note of finality Ginny wasn't willing to capitulate. She squirmed a little in her seat as she faced her mother across the breakfast table in the guest house where they were staying in Ballytor. As she'd pointed out more than once already any act of cruelty to a horse was her concern: it should be the concern of *any* normal, sensitive, intelligent person. Her mother, however, was firmly opposed to any action that could possibly be construed as 'prying into other people's affairs'.

'But, Mum, an act of cruelty to a horse – or any animal – *is* my business,' she insisted. 'You can't just see it and not do anything about it. That's cowardice, or worse.'

'My dearest daughter, you don't *know* that it was cruel. Keeping a horse in running water could very well be some form of treatment, some special equine therapy. In different countries people have different ways of doing things. You yourself said before we came here that the Irish are experts when it comes to horses.'

Ginny sensed she was being out-manœuvred. 'Well, I've never heard of anything quite so *callous* as that – to leave a horse, all on its own, for hours on end – '

'Oh, Ginny, we're not going over all that again! You admit you don't know how long the horse was in the stream and it had gone when you returned. It might have been there a very short time, from just before you found him and then dashed off to Skel-whatever-it-is. You really must keep a sense of proportion in these matters.'

'But something *sinister* is going on, Mum, I'm positive,' Ginny persisted. 'Carmen more or less said so – well, hinted, anyway.'

'Probably just her manner with a stranger. And we are strangers here, just remember that. I don't like the idea of your going round upsetting the locals, so steer clear of trouble, if only for my sake. We've got enough troubles of our own with this play.'

'Oh, is Maggy Nuisance still trying to run the show?'

'*Who?*'

'Well, that's what Mr Anderson calls her,' said Ginny hastily, striving not to giggle. 'Has Mrs Anderson recovered?'

'Enough to make some of us wish she hadn't!' Jane Luellen remarked with unusual asperity. She picked up her script from beside her plate. 'Look, Ginny, there are some lines I've just *got* to concentrate on before I go down to the hall this morning. Didn't you say you were going to write your postcards?'

Ginny nodded. 'And then I thought I'd do some real exploring, courtesy of Mr McCormick's private cycling club.'

'Yes, well, all right, but please don't start trying to rescue the entire horse population of western Ireland. And you will be at the dress rehearsal tonight, won't you? By then I shall really need some family support.'

'Wouldn't miss that for anything,' promised the actress's daughter.

When she found that the grey horse was not standing in the stream for the second day in succession Ginny's first reaction was one of profound relief; but there was also just the merest tinge of disappointment for she'd been relishing the

47

thought of actually cutting him free from his bonds.

Still, she could now go and see him at the stables where he lived – just so long as she could find them. Today, however, she had a good idea where to start looking. Once again, it was Mr McCormick, the Ballytor shopkeeper, who had proved really helpful. When visiting him, an hour or so earlier, to stock up for another picnic, Ginny, as casually as possible, had mentioned her great interest in birds (particularly seabirds) and horses (especially racehorses). Someone, she added, had told her that there was a man who trained racehorses not very far away: but she couldn't quite remember the name – 'Caff-er-something,' she thought.

'Cafferkey that'll be,' supplied Mr McCormick. 'Has a place just the other side of Skelhouley and indeed he does keep a horse or two. Not anything that'll win the Derby on three legs, though, from what I hear!'

Rather to Mr McCormick's surprise, that little joke was greeted by Ginny with a peal of laughter. But then, he wasn't to know that she was really expressing her delight in the way her ploy had worked: for she had guessed that he was just the sort of man who would know everybody and everything that went on in the surrounding country.

'Cafferkey's not the man for the visitors, I'm

thinking,' the shopkeeper went on. 'Doesn't like company of any sort, really. Ye'll be finding the seagulls an' all the more attractive!'

When she laughed at that, too, he promptly produced a pair of binoculars and insisted that she borrow them 'to see the creatures at their best, wheeling up and down the sky'. Really, Ginny told herself as she left and rode off again on his bike, he's the most *miraculous* man I could ever have found.

Because she hadn't wanted even Mr McCormick to know too much of what was in her mind she hadn't sought directions from him as to the whereabouts of Cafferkey's place. In any case, as it was 'just the other side of Skelhouley' it shouldn't be hard to find. If necessary, she could always ask someone, though she didn't want to risk drawing attention to her interest in the grey horse.

From the moorland, she free-wheeled down towards the town, feeling very content with life. She was in no doubt at all that she would very soon be re-united with Grey Horse (what *was* his name? she wondered constantly) and that he would relish every bite of the apples and mints she had bought for him. So far as she could tell there was no easy way of skirting Skelhouley. Hoping that she wouldn't be spotted by Carmen, who would surely guess her mission, she pedalled steadfastly along the street, looking neither left nor right. And she was in luck: not even the man with the walking stick was in view.

On the far side of the town the road began to rise, though not very steeply, and then became a series of loosely connected bends. Over to her right, hills divided by steep-sided valleys climbed ahead of her. Her progress was slow for she was looking out for any sign at all of a farm or small-holding with accompanying stable-block. Buildings, though, were rare and she was beginning to think that, somehow, she had chosen the wrong route when she spotted a pair of leaning gateposts. They looked incongruous because they supported no gate and the dirt track between them just wandered away haphazardly over the brow of a low hill. But, attached to one of the posts, was a deal board bearing the one word: Cafferkey. It appeared to have been inscribed with the end of a hot poker.

Her heart thumping with excitement and apprehension, Ginny laid the cycle down in the long grass just off the road. Then, very slowly, she walked up the track.

The house, when she caught her first glimpse of it, appeared ordinary enough: long, low and whitewashed and fairly typical for a farming community. Attached to it was a line of other buildings, all of different heights, and Ginny supposed that at least one of them contained the stables. On the unfenced

50

land in front of the farm sheep were grazing in company with half a dozen cows, all, oddly enough, in assorted colours. In the gentle sunlight of the morning it was a peaceful scene.

Ginny was wondering how near she dare approach the property without risk of being spotted when, from the side of the house, a man appeared: and he was leading a grey horse. In her mind there was no doubt at all that it was the same horse that she had seen tethered in the stream. Her pulse quickened again, but she remained stock-still, praying that she hadn't been noticed. But the man turned away to go round towards the rear of the buildings. The horse was already saddled and Ginny felt certain that it was about to be ridden: and that was something she keenly wanted to see.

Behind the house the hill rose very sharply again and the facing slope was quite well wooded: from up there, she should have a perfect view of any gallop that was going to take place and the trees themselves would provide her with all the concealment she needed.

She raced back to the road, grabbed the binoculars out of the saddle-bag, hauled the cycle into the cover of the hedge and then, as fast as she dared, made her way across the adjoining field. Her luck was in, for there was a fold in the ground that was almost parallel to the edge of Cafferkey's land. It was a strain on her legs, and particularly her knees, to move at speed while bent low, but she was prepared to put up with that so long as she remained out of sight of the farm.

The going became harder still when she met the face of the hill, but because she was now presumably ahead of the man and horse, it was more important than ever to keep her head down. Ginny was thankful she was wearing a dark green T-shirt and jeans instead of the white shirt and shorts she'd so very nearly chosen that morning. Steeling herself not to look back until she had reached some cover, she forced herself up the gradient towards the trees and bushes. When she paused to take a few deep breaths she began to think about the man: was it Cafferkey himself? At that range it had been impossible to guess at his age, but his build was fairly slight and she had the impression that he was rather bow-legged.

At last, halfway up the hill, she deemed it safe to have a look at the scene below. Planting herself behind a birch tree, she couldn't at first spot the grey horse. Then she saw them, much further away than she'd expected them to be. For the man had mounted and was heading away from the farm; fortunately, however, the horse was moving at no more than a gentle canter and, quickly, Ginny was able to bring them into focus with the glasses. The image was so sharp that, to Ginny's eyes, horse and rider seemed no more than a few yards away from her. As they crossed the undulating pastureland at the base of the hill there was no suggestion at all that they were having anything more than a pleasant and effortless spell of exercise. All the same, if they continued much further in that direction, Ginny realised to her dismay, they would very soon be out of her sight.

Then, with a very swift turn, the grey was being urged into a gallop. Within a few strides he was turning again – and this time was being driven straight up the hill. Ginny was astonished by such a procedure . . . but not too astonished to be aware of the zest with which the grey seemed to be tackling his task.

The rider, beautifully balanced, had the mannerisms and all the style of a professional jockey. That, however, didn't surprise her at all: most trainers of racehorses had been jockeys in their time and by now she was convinced that the man riding the grey was Cafferkey himself.

As soon as the horse began to falter against the increasing severity of the climb his rider quickly wheeled him about. 'Oh, thank goodness for that,' Ginny murmured. She was relieved that the horse wasn't being stretched to his limit again by a man she was convinced was a sadist.

Now, while the grey cantered over the pasture-land again, Ginny traversed the distant scene with her binoculars and then, quite idly, began to study the lay-out of the farm buildings. Just as she'd imagined, the long, low-roofed building attached to the house itself was the stable block and from her present vantage point she was able to look directly into it. Which, she wondered, was the box that belonged to the grey? She examined each one in turn, but she could pick up no clue from any of them: so far as she could tell, they were all identical.

Momentarily, she switched her interest back to horse and rider, but at that moment they were doing nothing out of the ordinary. Her gaze returned to the farm – and she was just in time to see a girl emerging from one of the boxes and leading out a horse. Involuntarily, Ginny's fingers tightened their grip on the binoculars. Until she had to lower them because of the pain they were causing her she hadn't even been aware of how hard she'd been pressing the eyepieces into her eye-sockets.

'I don't believe it,' she told herself. 'I just DO NOT believe it!'

She shook her head in the hope of clearing away confusion and then, raising the glasses to her eyes once more focused again on that astonishing sight.

For the horse now being walked round and

round in the stable yard was absolutely identical to the one that Mr Cafferkey was riding at that moment. The conformation and colouring were exactly the same, even to the much darker patch of grey just behind the saddle.

To the layman, two horses of the same colour, whether they were chestnuts or bays or greys, often looked alike unless they possessed some obvious distinguishing features, such as white socks or a blaze. But Ginny was so used to working with horses that no two ever looked alike to her: every one was an individual with its own markings and colour shades. Although she had spent very little time with the grey when he was standing in the stream she'd been confident she'd know him again anywhere. That confidence had now evaporated completely.

Her binoculars began to move like a metronome, swinging back and forth between the horse in the open and the horse in the yard. It was the uniformity of the colour that made it so difficult to separate them; apart from that darker area on the hindquarters there were no distinctive markings at all. Of course, if they'd been standing side by side it might just have been easier to decide which was the horse she'd met: in that situation she might have found a vital clue in temperament. *Her* grey, as she thought of him, was so calm and relaxed and it was unlikely that his 'twin' would be so placid. There was even a possibility that *her* horse would recognize her, brief though their acquaintance had been.

Gradually she began to concentrate her attention on the horse in the stable yard. It had become evident to her that he was walking rather feelingly on his near fore, as if it caused him pain or discomfort to put his weight on that leg. Had he, perhaps, injured it recently?

A minute or two later Ginny's deduction appeared to be confirmed. The girl leading him halted the horse and then ran her hand down his foreleg as if feeling for evidence of a trouble spot. From Richard McDade at Plumtree Lane Stables, Ginny had learned something of the 'leg troubles' that bedevilled every racehorse trainer at one time or another. Often enough, the problem was the tendons in a horse's forelegs: tendons that were no thicker than a man's thumb and yet had to withstand the pressure of about half a ton of horse when landing over an obstacle at a speed of up to 40 miles per hour. If those tendons are strained, perhaps as a result of over-exertion or a sudden, sharp turn while out at exercise, inflammation sets up – inflammation that was revealed to the horse's handler through a feeling of 'heat' in the affected leg. In that situation a horse had to be rested and not

57

resume training for at least a week. If the 'heat' signals were not spotted in time or ignored then the animal would eventually go lame and, if required to jump, might then very well tear the tendon.

It seemed to Ginny that the girl gave a shake of her head as she straightened up after inspecting the grey's near-fore and, sure enough, after one more turn round the yard the animal was led back into his box. Automatically, Ginny reverted to watching the other grey, the one she believed now was not *her* horse. And there wasn't any doubt about *his* fitness. Once more, he was charging up the slope with great zest. She began to wish that his rider would give him a rest so that she could study the animal in greater detail when he was stationary. Then, perhaps, she would be able to find some differences between the two greys.

Ginny decided that she needed a break, too. Her eyes were beginning to ache from so much avid viewing. She lowered the binoculars, blinked a couple of times and was just about to look for a place to sit when someone spoke.

'Well, now, I can see that you like watching the horses. Don't you think he goes well, that one?'

The voice was so startlingly close that Ginny gasped even before she turned round. Then, when she saw what the man was carrying, her hand flew

to her mouth to stifle another exclamation as she pressed her back against the tree that had shielded her for so long. Held loosely in the crook of his right arm was a shotgun.

It was only when she realized that the weapon was pointed at the ground, not at herself, that Ginny looked into the man's face – and saw that he was no more than a boy, hardly taller than herself, pale and thin-faced with a lock of dark hair falling across his left eye. Belying the presence of the shotgun, his gaze was quizzical, almost amused: not hostile at all.

'What – what did you say?' Ginny asked, struggling to recover her nerve. Was he a gamekeeper or a warden of some kind, justified in challenging her about trespassing? If so, he was adopting a very casual attitude, leaning his shoulder against the trunk of a tree a few metres further up the hillside.

'I was just observing that you were very interested in the horse at exercise.'

'Oh yes,' replied Ginny, rather liking his use of observing, a word that not many English boys would have employed. 'I'm really very fond of horses.' She paused, then added: 'He looks a real racehorse. That's Mr Cafferkey riding him, isn't it?'

When the boy nodded Ginny felt a surge of satisfaction that her ruse had worked. Already she was

60

regaining her composure after the shock of being confronted with a shotgun. Her recently adopted policy of taking the initiative in strange encounters was paying dividends, she decided.

'What's his name – the grey, I mean?'

'That'll be Cormac now,' said the boy with a sudden grin that was as wide as it was unexpected.

'Oh, what a coincidence! I've just got to know somebody called McCormick – almost the same name.'

'Donal McCormick, that'll be – the storekeeper in Ballytor, I'm thinking.'

'That's right,' Ginny agreed, taken aback again. 'Does everybody know everybody around here?'

'That we do. It's a very small population we have. Not much work here, so if people haven't a job, well, they go off somewhere to find it. The ones that stay, we know all about. Ginny, that's your name, isn't it?'

'Goodness, yes it is! But how did you know? I mean, I don't think even Mr McCormick knows that.' The initiative she thought was firmly in her grasp had slipped away.

The boy's grin was becoming a fixture. 'Well, there aren't many visitors from England around here at present – not in Skelhouley, anyway – and not as many as that, I'm thinking, interested in a grey horse. But, ye see, my sister met one yesterday and this girl said her name was Ginny. So I'm betting heavily on you being the one.'

Ginny couldn't help smiling. She liked his style. 'Oh, I see. So your sister is Carmen. You're not all that much alike, are you? By the way, what's your name?'

'Martin.' His pronunciation, however, turned it into Mart'n.

'Well, Martin, would you do something for me? Would you please point that gun in another direction? I'm afraid guns are not my thing. Anyway, what are you carrying it for?'

He broke it open to show her that the gun wasn't loaded. 'I was thinking I might shoot something for the pot – rabbit, a hare, anything that'll taste good. We don't all shoot people, whatever you think about the Irish.'

'I thought you were stalking me! Sorry, Martin. But, you see, I never heard you at all until you spoke.'

'Ah, well now, you learn to move quietly among horses, so's not to disturb them. Thoroughbreds are excitable creatures. Anything sudden or out of the ordinary is inclined to startle 'em, upset them. But then, you'll be knowing about all that, won't you?'

'Oh, you work with racehorses! Is that with Mr Cafferkey? Are you the stable jockey, Martin?'

That news so thrilled Ginny that she hadn't really listened to his last few words.

'I don't ride as often as I'd like to. The guv'nor – Cafferkey himself – well, he doesn't have many horses, ye see. So the opportunities for a good rider aren't there. That stable's not the place for a man of ambition. Over the water, ye see, there's always an opening, if you can find the right contact, make the right connection. Lots of Irish jockeys have made it right to the top in England – Tommy Stack, Jonjo O'Neill, fellas like that. You just need to be given the chance, that's the big thing, Ginny.'

She nodded. The only jockey she'd met was Gavin Greene, who rode Tamela and other horses for Richard McDade, and he was English. But Mr McDade was Irish-born and she knew that he had started as a rider in his own country before setting up as a trainer in the Cotswolds.

'Is the grey, Cormac, one of the horses that you do for Mr Cafferkey?' she asked, keen to turn the conversation back to horses.

'Ye might say so,' he answered, rather cryptically Ginny thought. 'Look, I think we'll have to be going now,' he went on hurriedly. 'The guv'nor'll be back any time and he'll be wanting a word. He's not the man to be kept waiting.'

'Yes, of course,' said Ginny, and together they began to make their way down the hillside. There

63

were several questions she'd have liked to ask but was uncertain how to phrase them. She sensed that there was something distinctly odd going on concerning the two greys but, for the moment, it might be wiser to steer clear of that subject. She had an idea, too, that it wasn't a coincidence that Martin had come upon her like that when she was watching the horses. Perhaps he himself had been sent up there by Cafferkey to keep an eye open for strangers while Cormac was being galloped. So far as she could tell, however, Martin wasn't aware that she had seen *both* horses. The second grey had already been taken back into his box before Martin spoke to her: just before that he'd probably been watching her rather than the stables – and, anyway, he was armed with a gun, not binoculars.

'You know,' she said, breaking the long silence as they approached the road where she'd left the bike, 'I'd really love to meet Cormac. He's a very attractive sort and he moves really well. I expect you've great plans for him, haven't you?'

Martin shrugged. 'Might be anything – ye can never tell until you put 'em to the test the hard way. But the guv'nor, well, he doesn't encourage people to go nosing round his stables. A very *secretive* man, he is, is Cafferkey.'

'Oh well, perhaps I'll see him again out in the open,' said Ginny brightly, adding: 'Even on the

64

moors, all on his own.' And she held her breath as soon as she'd spoken.

The look he gave her was calculating: and then he ran a thumbnail across his teeth. 'Well now,' he said eventually, 'you could be seeing him the day after tomorrow if you liked. He's running at the Junction – a bumper race over two miles.'

'The Junction, what's that?' Ginny asked bewilderedly. 'And what's a bumper race, for heaven's sake?'

'The Junction, ah well now, that's our nearest racecourse. Killwaylow Junction, a few miles down the road from Ballytor. A bumper race is for the amateur riders, did you not know that?'

'No, no, they're not called that in England, I'm sure. But, Martin, I'd love to see Cormac run. So I'll definitely be there.'

'That's good then. I'll be looking out for you, Ginny. There's things I'd like to be talking to you about.'

'Right. See you there, then, Martin.'

By which time, she reflected as she rode away, she intended to be better informed about the subjects *she* wanted to discuss.

Five

Killwaylow Junction was like no racecourse Ginny had ever seen; and certainly like none she would ever have imagined. For a start, the entrance seemed to be by way of a farmyard, cobbled and narrow and reeking most distinctly of agricultural remains of one kind or another. To the rear of the farm buildings, which were in a state of semi-dereliction, was the structure that she supposed could very loosely be described as the grandstand: anyway, there was nothing else that could possibly serve that purpose. It consisted of long rows of wooden planking, one stepped up behind the other, under a corrugated metal roof that, in places, had simply rusted away to leave large holes with jagged edges. Fortunately, it was another sunny day and so the patrons using the stand were in no danger at present of a drenching: though what risks they took just by standing on those sagging planks was another matter altogether.

The winning post, at least, was plainly recognizable and it still amused Ginny to think of it as the 'jam stick', which was what Richard McDade called it. The runners would, quite literally, come up to the winning post because it was set on the edge of a very considerable dip in the track. An even deeper depression occurred on the far side of the oval-shaped course. 'When they go down into that you'll be lucky to see even the tops of the jockeys' caps from the grandstand,' Mr McCormick forecast. 'When they come out of that hollow they start on the last, swinging bend, so you can just imagine the sort of jiggery-pokery that goes on down there!'

Ginny gazed across in that direction, having no trouble at all in dreaming up dire happenings in the hollow, but her view was somewhat obscured by a collection of animals grazing imperturbably in the very centre of the course: cattle, sheep and even a few donkeys. The arrival of the most excitable racegoers – and a large crowd was building up quickly – was having no effect at all on their feeding habits.

'It's a popular belief that some of those donkeys out there can run a deal faster than a few of the horses ye'll be seeing today,' remarked Mr McCormick, noting Ginny's particular field of interest. 'I'll just be hoping that *our* horse isn't in that category!'

'Oh, Mr McCormick, have you no faith at all in my judgement?' she replied laughingly. 'I *told* you, Cormac can go like the wind, even when he's racing uphill. So this course should suit him down to the ground – er, if you see what I mean!'

'Ginny, I wish you wouldn't be addressing me so formally. Mr McCormick indeed! Everyone who knows me calls me Donny. So couldn't you be using that name, too? Especially now that we've become such friends. I mean, its no longer just a business relationship, buying and selling and so on now is it?'

'No, of course it isn't! I never though of it like that, anyway, even the first time I came into your shop. You were so helpful and friendly and – well, I just feel we've been friends for years already. So it was absolutely perfect when you said you'd like to come to the races with me. No, *escort* – that was the word you used, wasn't it?'

The previous day Ginny, seeking information about the Killwaylow meeting, had naturally gone to Mr McCormick as a proved reliable source. Just as naturally, she'd mentioned that she was particularly interested in a horse that bore a name very similar to his own. She wasn't at all surprised to learn that he'd already heard something about Cormac.

68

'In Ireland, where racehorses are concerned, there's always a rumour flying around. Especially in small communities like this one. Some people hear one thing, some another. But the talk never stops ... talk, talk, talk about horses all the day long with some people. I was hearing that this Cormac is a nice enough animal, might even be better than that one day. Run only once, down at Mallow, finished down the field, but that's traditional with a first outing. Means nothing except that he's now got a bit of experience behind him.'

That was the extent of Mr McCormick's knowledge of the horse, but as Ginny had supposed, he was informative about other matters, too. He explained that a bumper race was so called because the amateur rider, unlike the experienced professional, was inclined to bump the saddle when galloping. Invariably, it was the last race of the day and was designed for horses that previously had not won; quite often, trainers of horses that had shown a lot of promise on home gallops, but had done nothing on a racecourse, would use such a race to bring off a gamble – provided they could rely on the skills of the amateur rider. Not infrequently, plenty of the other runners wouldn't be trying very hard anyway: they'd be running solely for the experience. But, added Mr McCormick, 'bumpers' could be very rough events to ride in because most of the amateurs were determined to score over their rivals in one way or another.

'You really know an awful lot about racing, don't you?' Ginny had remarked – and received the grinning reply: 'Show me the Irishman who *doesn't* have a bit of interest in the horses!' Then, to her delight, he'd said that, if she'd allow him that pleasure, he'd be very happy to escort her to the Killwaylow meeting.

'Oh, I'd be putting up the shutters on the store, anyway,' he said, correctly interpreting the reason for her surprised look. 'People round here treat the Junction races as a bit of a festival, an excuse for a day out. So I won't be missing any business by closing for the day. I'm thinking, too, that if your Cormac is as smart as you say, well, it could be more profitable than selling half the shop!'

They'd arrived at the Junction in style, for Donny McCormick's car turned out to be a Mercedes, which was a fair indication of how successful his business enterprises were: the store in Ballytor, it appeared, was only one of them, but so far Ginny hadn't discovered exactly what his other 'lines' were. She was glad to be in his company for several reasons. For one thing, she was rather apprehensive about meeting Martin again: she couldn't help feeling that there was something sinister about him, something that had nothing at all to do with the fact that he'd been carrying a gun on their first encounter. For another, she desperately wanted to talk to someone about Cormac.

So far she'd confided nothing to Donny about her discovery of the horse tethered in the stream or of seeing that Cafferkey had in his stable two apparently identical greys. First, she wanted to see Cormac for herself, in close-up, in the parade ring before the bumper race. That was the time to start asking questions. In the meantime, she'd just have to be patient – and enjoy the first five races on the card.

'Well, now, Ginny, if you think you've got the feel of the place after that long look round, shall we go and look at a few horses?' asked Donny, breaking into her thoughts. 'Let's see if you can find the equal of that Tamela you were telling me all about. Sure, a winner is what we need to get us off to the best start possible.'

Together they strolled past the ramshackle grandstand to a parade ring that really was almost completely circular in design with just one gap in the rail through which the horses could be admitted and depart. The first race of the afternoon, a steeplechase for novices run over two miles, was to be contested by eight runners and already three of them were circulating in the company of their handlers. As she studied them Ginny was

71

remembering the time when she had led Tamela round the parade ring at Pershore before he went off to win his first race over hurdles. She had felt then that every eye must be on her alone even though common sense told her that the spectators were interested only in the horses. None of the present batch of stable lads and girls appeared at all self-conscious and one or two were whispering fervently to their charges, perhaps to encourage them to produce their best form as soon as they stretched out on the track.

'So, which one is it to be?' asked Donny, breaking in on her thoughts.

'Oh, er, I haven't made my mind up yet,' she answered hastily and more or less truthfully.

'Well, maybe you'll get a bit of a clue from the names and the form,' he suggested with a grin, handing her a racecard. 'Now, just be taking your time, Ginny, because I'm relying on your expertise in these matters. Those bookmakers are rich enough without requiring any contributions from my pocket.'

She didn't care to admit it to many people, but often enough its name influenced her in choosing a horse to follow. It had to be a sensible name and it had to sound right: horses with 'silly' names such as Fish'n'Chips or Twerp, very seldom turned out to be much good on the racecourse or anywhere else. So she scanned the list of runners on the card and decided that two in particular ought to be worth looking at: Mr Biggles and Trilogy.

Ginny pointed them out to Donny, who nodded approvingly at the mention of her second choice. 'Trilogy, now, he's got a bit of form – fourth and then second in his two races so far. Just getting the hang of things, maybe. Could be third time lucky – *ought* to be with a name like that!'

'Oh, yes, that's a lovely coincidence,' Ginny smiled. 'But I still think I prefer Mr Biggles. Look, that's him over there on the far side of the ring: that very dark chestnut with the sheepskin nose-band. Very deep-chested – and that means he's got plenty of heart-room and courage. At least, that's what Mr McDade says. And he's got a wonderful sheen to his coat so he must be fit. Yes, I think he's the one, Donny. I hope he's a good price.'

'Should be at that,' remarked her companion, studying the racecard again. 'Only had one run and didn't finish in the first four that time. Maybe he was one of those just running for the experience that time. Well, come on then, let's be seeing what those old rogues will be offering us.'

He was, as Ginny supposed, referring to the bookmakers; but those gentlemen of the prices were apparently in no hurry to start trading as she and Donny discovered on reaching their line of

73

business stands. Only a couple had chalked up prices; the rest seemed to be waiting for inspired information to reach them from various mysterious sources. Meanwhile they were filling the interval by muttering darkly to their clerks, who had pencils poised over large ledger sheets on which eventually bets would be recorded.

'Ah, it's just as I thought,' Donny murmured with assumed disillusionment, 'they're making my old horse the favourite. Just look at that, now: 6–4 Trilogy. So who could be getting rich on that sort of investment?'

'Better a short-priced winner than a long-priced loser – that's what they always say,' Ginny remarked with airy wisdom.

Donny raised his eyebrows at that piece of advice and, as if sensing that Trilogy might soon shorten even further in price, stepped up to one of the bookmakers to hand over some money. Ginny couldn't see exactly how much he put on, but plainly it was enough to worry the bookie, who promptly erased the 6–4 and substituted 5–4. Oh gosh, Ginny thought despairingly, I hope Donny won't blame me if he loses all that.

As soon as she saw someone put a price against the name of Mr Biggles she moved in to place her own £1 on the horse at 8–1. But Donny held out a restraining arm. 'Don't rush your fences, Ginny,' he advised. 'I think that's the right phrase in the circumstances. You just might be getting longer odds in a minute. With outsiders these fellas often just chuck a price on the board to see what happens.'

Sure enough, a few moments later she spotted that another bookmaker was offering Mr Biggles at 10–1. After watching as many boards as she could for a little while she decided that she wasn't going to get better odds than that. Her bet went on and she pocketed the slip of cardboard the bookie gave her.

When the runners left the paddock and cantered down to the start Ginny followed Mr Biggles' progress through the binoculars. The dark chestnut moved with a nice, easy stride, his head held well down in the style of a horse that knows very well how to take care of itself during a race. She'd decided as Mr Biggles went past her that he had a kind eye, but she refrained from mentioning that to Donny: she didn't want her friend to think that mere sentiment was another of the reasons that governed her choice.

Trilogy was a fairly flashy light chestnut with three white socks and his jockey was having a hard task to restrain him as they sped down the track. By now Trilogy was an even warmer favourite at evens and Donny was looking well pleased with himself at having secured a longer price for his money. A rangy bay called Turncoat was the second favourite at 9–2 while Mr Biggles was still 10–1.

'Come on, Ginny,' said her friend, taking her comfortably by the arm, 'let's go and watch the melodrama.'

He led the way to one of the upper rows of the rickety grandstand. Ginny looked around, and then up at the roof, warily, but so far as she could tell Donny had chosen a relatively safe spot. Moments before the race was due to start she noticed a surge of punters descend upon the line of bookmakers: it was as if every one of them had been given last-minute and truly inspired information about the winner and was determined to strike the bet of a lifetime. Donny was watching the prices fluctuate on the boards and, turning to Ginny, murmured: 'Seems as if there's a bit of late money for your old nag. Down to 8–1 he is, now.'

She nodded, not wanting to break her concentration on the runners circling by the starter's rostrum. Mr Biggles looked thoroughly relaxed and, when the white flag dropped, his rider tucked him in at the rear of the field. None of the runners was keen to set a strong pace, but eventually a lightly framed grey took over the lead. Although she knew that in any race one horse very seldom led from start to finish Ginny immediately experienced misgivings about having completely ignored this particular front-runner when making her choices. Greys, it seemed to her, were tending to dominate her life at present.

By the second fence, however, the grey, pecking badly on landing, had surrendered the lead to Turncoat. Mr Biggles took both obstacles fluently, even effortlessly, and Ginny's sense of alarm disappeared as quickly as it had come. Trilogy, taking off far too soon at the second jump, only just survived it and she risked a glance at Donny to see how he was reacting to such a mistake by his choice. But Donny appeared unperturbed despite the fact that Trilogy was now trailing the field by several lengths. As they approached the next fence Mr Biggles was fourth of the eight runners.

As if determined not to allow Turncoat to build up a lead the grey's jockey shook up his mount and went off in pursuit of the second favourite. Soon the pair were matching strides and the pace quickened noticeably as they pulled well ahead of the third horse. Turncoat seemed not to approve of having his leadership challenged and, as they came into the fifth obstacle, an open ditch, his rider hardly needed to give him a slap down the neck for the bay to put in a huge leap.

Turncoat cleared the fence in majestic style. But,

in trying to emulate his rival, the grey took off a fraction too soon, crashed heavily through the birch obstacle and catapulted his rider from the saddle.

Involuntarily Ginny joined in the chorus of excited 'Oh's' from the spectators and watched anxiously for the grey to struggle to his feet on the other side of the fence. As he did so he impeded another horse as it landed and its rider, too, was unable to keep his seat.

By now Turncoat was the best part of ten lengths clear of the second horse, Mr Biggles, and heading into the notorious dip at the furthest point on the course from the grandstand. Switching her attention back to the scene of the disaster Ginny saw, with relief, that the grey appeared to be quite unharmed by his mishap and that, after lying prone for several seconds, the jockey was now getting to his feet as a couple of medical attendants rushed towards him. The second jockey who'd come off had managed to keep hold of the reins and was preparing to re-mount, though by now he had no chance at all of catching any of the remaining six runners.

As the runners came into the final sweeping bend Ginny noted joyfully that Mr Biggles was closing the gap. Turncoat was no longer coasting along: his jockey was beginning to niggle at him to keep galloping. By the time the leader took the third last fence Mr Biggles was only a couple of lengths behind and still going very easily. Ginny started to think of what she would do with her winnings.

Around her the crowd was beginning to shout excitedly as, with just two fences to jump, the leaders were neck and neck. All eyes were on them, for it appeared that the remainder of the field were out of it unless complete disaster overtook both Turncoat and Mr Biggles. The bay was now being

81

driven along to maintain his marginal advantage, but still the jockey had scarcely moved on Mr Biggles. They rose together at the penultimate obstacle but, with Turncoat stumbling on landing, it was Mr Biggles who forged ahead.

'Go on, Mr Biggles, go on!' Ginny urged under her breath and the chestnut seemed to answer her call instantly. Turncoat was plainly flagging and then, as she glanced back, Ginny saw that the favourite was simply *sprinting* after the leading pair. Trilogy's backers, too, had caught sight of the chestnut's sudden, and startling, acceleration. He was catching Turncoat with every stride.

Under pressure Turncoat barely managed to scramble over the final fence and Trilogy passed him in the air. Mr Biggles was still half a dozen lengths ahead, but after a worried glance over his shoulder at the looming danger, his jockey sat down to ride for all he was worth. The roars of the crowd were reaching a crescendo as the favourite, seemingly still only cruising, rapidly reduced the leeway. The run-in was fairly short but, sweeping past Mr Biggles as though he was stationary, Trilogy had two lengths to spare at the winning post. Turncoat, running on gamely, managed to hold on to third place.

'Phew, I thought I was going to win that easily,' said Ginny. 'But Trilogy is some horse to come through like that. Well done, Donny. You must have landed a nice bet.'

Donny nodded, obviously well pleased with himself. 'Ah, I was thinking that the jockey had left it a bit late to set him about his business. But, sure, he won very snugly in the end.'

'Oh, what a lovely word! I've never heard that in England – we'd always say that a horse won comfortably. Your way is *much* nicer.'

Donny smiled and said he thought he should go and collect his winnings before the bookies ran out of money. Because Trilogy had been such a warm favourite it took some minutes for Donny to get his cash and, meanwhile, Ginny enjoyed herself listening to snatches of conversation among the crowd. The comment she came to treasure wa made by a florid-featured farmer-type who was telling a gathering of sympathetic listeners: 'Ye can judge how far my luck's out – there's a bird's nest in my champagne bucket!' He sounded as if he meant it, too. It seemed to Ginny that practically everyone knew everyone else on the course and the atmosphere was a great deal merrier and more in-formal than she'd experienced at any English racecourse. Of course, the success of the favourite in the opening race probably had a good deal to do with that.

'Well, now, you put me on to the first winner

so what about making it a double?' Donny asked genially as he returned to her side. 'But, this time, I hope you're going to back it, too.'

So, once more, they went to study the runners in the parade ring. Donny was positive that the only advice he'd rely on was hers; now that he was so much in pocket she didn't mind taking the responsibility of making the choice for the next bet. The second race was a handicap, run over two and a half miles, for hurdlers, and after watching them walk round several times Ginny declared that she'd narrowed down her selection to two: a roan called Crack Shot and a dark chestnut named Meticulous. It was hard to make a final choice but, prompted by Donny, she eventually settled for Meticulous.

'That's good enough for me,' grinned Donny. 'As it happens, though, I'm inclined to agree with your choice. Maybe we should have a bit of a saver on Crack Shot, too, just to widen the interest, you'll understand.'

Meticulous proved to be second favourite at 3–1, but Crack Shot, clearly totally unfancied, could be backed at various prices between 16–1 and 25–1. Donny placed his own and Ginny's bets at the most favourable rates and then they returned to what Ginny had decided was their 'lucky' place in the grandstand. They soon knew their fate with Crack Shot when he made a complete hash of the second hurdle, sprawled, almost fell and dropped right out of the race. By halfway, he'd been pulled up.

'Not surprised about that one,' remarked Donny casually, still watching the race. 'I remember now that he had terrible leg trouble last season. They must have tried everything to get him right, but in the paddock I thought the treatment hadn't done the trick.'

Ginny's interest quickened. 'What sort of treatment would they try, Donny?'

'Oh, all sorts, even running cold water, though that's a bit drastic sometimes. If the animal races too soon the tendon might snap altogether, then it's an operation it needs. Look, Ginny, our fella's moving up very nicely.'

So many thoughts were whirling through her head that it was a moment or two before Ginny could concentrate again on the race. Then, focusing her glasses on the leading group, she saw that Meticulous, easily identified by his jockey's green-and-orange check colours had indeed come up smoothly on the outside of the field. The favourite, a good-looking bay called Claret-and-Gold, was keeping him company on the heels of the leading trio and it looked as if the jockeys on the two principal market fancies were worried only about each other.

By the time they came into the home straight

neither had made a significant forward move. In unison they jumped the last hurdle, where one of the leaders fell awkwardly, interfering with another of the front-runners. Suddenly the whips rose and fell and, still stride for stride, Claret-and-Gold and Meticulous powered into the lead.

On the run-in first one and then the other seemed to gain the advantage, to the almost delirious delight of the crowd. Then, with a final heave of his arms, the jockey in the green-and-orange hurled his mount across the line.

'Ah, that's just terrific!' yelled Donny, seizing his young partner in a hug that threatened to crack bones. 'You've done it again, Ginny!'

In fact, it was some moments before the official announcement confirmed what he'd seen: that Meticulous had won by a short-head. In the interim some bookies were betting that the result would be a dead-heat.

Ginny, almost as overcome by excitement as Donny, was happy to race round to the unsaddling enclosure to greet the winner and admire him anew at close quarters. Donny was all for buying a bottle of champagne to celebrate their success until Ginny explained that even friendly Irish policemen might not approve of her drinking under-age! Actually, although priests were plentiful there wasn't a policeman to be seen.

86

By the fifth race, Donny himself was in a distinctly sober mood and Ginny remarked that it was perhaps as well that he hadn't spent any of his winnings on a celebration. After Meticulous' success their luck had changed completely and they hadn't found another winner: one of their selections had even fallen at the final fence with the race apparently at his mercy.

They were on their now familiar route to the parade ring when a woman in a dazzling light blue outfit hailed Donny enthusiastically. 'Oh, calamity!' he whispered in an aside to Ginny. 'An old flame – but cold as yesterday's breakfast now. Still, I'll have to have a word.' So saying, he stepped forward to greet her with the sort of heartiness that ought to have sounded false even to her: 'Good day, Bernadette, and sure what a pleasure it is to be seeing you again....'

Suppressing a strong desire to laugh aloud at Donny's obvious discomfort, Ginny stepped to one side and sauntered off towards the horses. Donny would know where to look for her when he escaped from Bernadette. Then, as she passed a narrow entrance to the racecourse stables, it was her turn to have a surprise encounter. For, as she glanced towards the row of loose boxes, she came face to face with Martin, the young man who worked for Cafferkey, the trainer of Cormac. Thankfully, Ginny

87

noted, on this occasion he wasn't carrying a shot-gun.

'Ah, Ginny,' he said, his face lighting up, 'I was just hoping to see you, that I was.'

'Good, I wanted to see you, too, Martin. How's Cormac? Is he going to win today?'

'Ah now, that's what I wanted to tell you.' His face suddenly lost its cheerfulness. 'Look, you mustn't be betting on him today, not at all. He'll not be winning this race.' His voice had dropped so that it was almost inaudible. 'But, please God, don't be telling anyone else about that. It's a secret between – between you and me, Ginny. Promise, now, you'll say not a word.'

'But why, Martin? What's wrong?' Ginny asked bewilderedly.

Worriedly he looked round as if to make sure that no one could possibly overhear them – and then, when he turned back to her, he ran a thumbnail along his teeth. 'The guv'nor would kill me if he knew I was telling you this,' he muttered. 'I daren't be telling you another thing. So – just forget Cormac today.'

Ginny couldn't leave it at that. She had to know more. 'Is he unfit? Has he injured a leg again?'

Martin didn't answer. He looked flabbergasted.

Six

'Come on, Martin, I want to know what's wrong,' Ginny persisted. She had more than an inkling, though, that already she'd hit on the truth. Martin's reaction to her shot in the dark made that fairly plain.

'How do you know about the injury?' It came out in a whisper.

'Because – because he was tethered in the stream on the moor, that's why.' One flash of insight was being followed by another. 'Martin, that's pretty drastic treatment, isn't it? Some horses I can think of couldn't stand it. And it looks as though it didn't work. It didn't, did it?'

Martin was now looking about him more frantically than ever. She guessed that he was fearful that Cafferkey, his guv'nor, was going to appear at any

89

moment. Ginny was beginning to feel sick with anger at what they'd done to that grey horse.

Suddenly Martin darted forward and grabbed her wrist before she could back away from him. 'But ye see, it nearly did work – Cormac's almost fine again. But the guv'nor daren't run – I mean, daren't take the risk. So well . . .' His voice trailed away.

'Let go!' Ginny tried to snatch her wrist out of his grip but he held her tenaciously. 'If you don't let go of my arm I'll –'

'Please, Ginny, just be listening one moment,' he urged. 'I can't explain now, but I will, I swear. After the last race. I must talk to you about – about England and things. I need your help. But now, I've got to see to the horse.'

'Martin whatever-your-name-is, I haven't the slightest intention of ever speaking to you again – about anything,' Ginny retorted in the coldest tone she could produce. 'You are – unspeakable!'

Before Martin could attempt any further pleadings a boy in a cloth cap came out of the stables and straight up to them. 'Been looking for you, Mart'n. Your boss wants you – fast.' And having delivered that message he shot a grin at Ginny and then departed.

The moment he released her wrist Ginny swung on her heel and walked away from him. She heard him call to her, but she didn't pause. But she was aware of the despair in his voice. 'After the last, Ginny – please. It's terr'bly important I talk to you.'

There was hardly any time at all for Ginny to reflect on that disturbing meeting with Martin for, almost immediately, Donal McCormick was back at her side. As he made no reference to Martin, Ginny assumed that Donny hadn't seen them together; for the moment, she wasn't inclined to mention the encounter. Donny was eager to 'get back on the winning trail', as he put it, but Ginny had little heart for picking out the winner of the fifth race. All her thoughts were concentrated on Cormac and the final race of the afternoon.

As it turned out, Donny managed to make a small profit by backing no fewer than three horses. Then he announced his intention of having 'the bet of a lifetime on your wonder horse, Cormac. Anyway, how can we possibly lose when it has a name like that?'

'Donny, I don't think that's a very good idea,' Ginny told him quietly. 'Before you decide about anything I want you to have a very, *very* careful look at him in the paddock. Then tell me if you think he's fit to run today – *really* fit in every way.'

'Ah, a premonition, is it? Hold your horses and all that?'

'Something like that,' Ginny agreed unsmilingly. 'Come on, he'll be parading now."

There were sixteen runners, the biggest field of the day, in the Junction Stakes, the last event of the day, and the majority of them were already walking round and round the ring. Cormac, however, was not among them. Trainers, owners and their friends and most of the riders were scattered in little groups all over the paddock, each speculating with solemn intensity on the chances of their own runner. Then, dramatically, Cormac made his entrance ... dramatically because, as his handler sought to find a space for him in the moving circle, a light-coloured filly, who'd been playing up for some moments, skitted sideways and almost cannoned into the newcomer.

Thoroughly alarmed, Cormac reared. Then, when he came down, it took all his handler's strength to prevent him from making a dash for freedom. The handler, as Ginny had expected, was Martin and it was a while before he was able to control the horse and introduce him into the ring. Even then Cormac was plainly far from happy about the situation and, though at last he consented to walk round, he was continuously tossing his head and changing his stride. If Martin had been hoping for another word with Ginny now his chance had gone: the grey demanded all his attention.

'Well, that one looks fresh enough,' remarked
Donny approvingly. 'Really full of beans.'

'Donny, look at his legs – as closely as you can.
Tell me what you think.'

Ginny's companion did as he was asked, but
after Cormac had made two circuits he reported

93

that he could see nothing wrong with the horse. 'Sound as a bell, he looks to me. What's troubling you, Ginny?'

'I'm not sure,' she had to admit. She realized that any horse was likely to react strongly to an unpleasant experience in unfamiliar surroundings, but the thing that had most impressed her about the grey in the stream was the calmness of his temperament.

It was when the horses were turned inwards and taken away to be united with their riders that Ginny remembered something. Whipping her binoculars up to her eyes she focused on Cormac's ears. Fortunately, he was facing her and so she was able to get an uninterrupted look at them. But what she was looking for, she didn't find. For when she had comforted the horse in the stream she had fondled his ears. Not every thoroughbred approved of that gesture, but the grey hadn't objected in any way at all. Her fingers had detected a tiny nick in the edge of one ear: it was a blemish of no significance, but to anyone who knew of its existence it was an identifying mark.

Cormac, the horse in the parade ring, had no such mark: both ears were flawless.

What that meant to Ginny was that the horse she was looking at now was not the horse she had seen in the stream. Whether he was the horse she had watched Cafferkey ride on the slopes behind his stables she had no way of knowing because she hadn't studied his ears then. Yet Martin hadn't denied – indeed, he'd more or less admitted – that Cormac, the horse running today, *was* the horse she'd seen standing in the stream. And Martin, before he realized what he was saying, had also confessed that the leg injury wasn't properly healed. Therefore . . .

'Ginny, is there something wrong with your hearing as well as with your eyesight?' Donny was asking her and, at the same time, gently jogging her elbow to secure her attention.

'Sorry – I was just, er, pondering something.'

'D'ye think I wasn't aware of that! Standing looking at a horse through glasses when he's but a few feet away from you – *and* not hearing a word I've been saying to you for the past five minutes! Now look, if we're going to make that fortune we've got to be moving – even the horses are on their way to the start.'

Still rather dazed by the conflicting ideas that were battering each other in her mind, Ginny followed him to where the bookmakers were drumming up business. She found it difficult at first to make sense of the prices that were shifting constantly, but one thing soon became clear: Cormac was one of the leading fancies. But, as she watched the shifting odds, his price was the one that steadily lengthened.

'I'm thinking you must have second sight,' Donny said in an awed tone. 'Cormac's really drifting, so somebody else knows something, too. It's Lightkeeper that's all the rage now. He's the one for me, all right.'

As if sensing that Ginny didn't want to bet, Donny descended on the nearest bookie, planted money in the man's hand, took his ticket and then silently led the way to the very top of the grandstand. Neither of them commented on whether their luck would be affected by a change of vantage point. As the horses began to line up for the start Ginny had a quick look again at the prices: although Cormac was now 7–2 he was still second favourite with Lightkeeper heading the market at 5–4. According to the bookies, it was a two-horse race, for at least 10–1 was freely available on any of the other runners.

Even before the horses came under starter's orders Ginny was sure she knew how the race was going to turn out. After only a furlong, Cormac went to the front. His rider, a Mr D. L. Wexton, made no effort to restrain his mount and appeared perfectly content to bob along a couple of lengths ahead of the next runner. Completing the first circuit they were still at the head of the field with the favourite, Lightkeeper, a very neatly made chestnut, handily placed in about fifth position.

Then, as the runners made their way down the far side of the course, Don't Hide, the filly who had been so fractious in the paddock, moved up to challenge for the lead. As if resenting her presence alongside him, Cormac lengthened his stride immediately and drew ahead again.

'Go on, Cormac, keep going!' Ginny urged fervently. In her heart, though, she knew he couldn't. Already the grey horse must have expended most, if not all, of his energy. Yet, as the runners descended the slope into the hollow, he was still in front by a clear length. She concentrated on watching the riders' caps and the blue-and-yellow of Mr Wexton continued in the van. Donny remained silent and Ginny had almost forgotten his presence beside her.

Then, as the runners made the final turn, Lightkeeper, to the delight of his many supporters, began a significant forward move. Mr Wexton was hard at work on Cormac, driving him for all he was worth towards the line, but it must have been as plain to him as it was to the crowd that his mount was a spent force. Lightkeeper sailed past him with effortless ease – and nothing was going to catch the favourite. Don't Hide rallied and was one of two runners to pass Cormac in the final furlong.

'Well now, I think you've real cause for complaint about the fate of your fellow,' Donny remarked sympathetically as Lightkeeper cruised past the post, the winner by a margin of six lengths. 'The jockey must have sawdust for brains. No horse can be expected to lead all the way over two miles on this course. 'Tis sheer madness to try it. He never even tried to give Cormac a breather at any stage!'

'I know,' Ginny agreed gloomily. 'They didn't seem to want him to win, did they? Still, *you* won again, Donny. I'm glad about that.'

'Glad enough to have dinner with me tonight to celebrate our great day?' he asked as they made their way down the steps. 'It would be the perfect way to end it, I'm thinking.'

'Oh well, yes, that would be lovely – if Mum doesn't mind. You see, it's her big day tomorrow and I should really be putting her through her paces. But maybe I can do that afterwards. She doesn't sleep much the night before a performance – *she* says.'

'Must be a bit like a winding-up gallop for a racehorse,' Donny grinned. 'Right, now, I'll be off for my winnings and then we'll fight our way out of here.'

Ginny had considered going to have a final look at Cormac but decided against it: she preferred to avoid another meeting with Martin. As they made their way through the crowds to the car park Donny chatted enthusiastically about the events of the afternoon, adding that in his opinion Cormac had shown a lot of potential and might be a very useful racehorse one day.

He was just unlocking the doors of the Mercedes when Ginny heard her name being spoken. She looked up and found Martin standing in front of her. 'Please read this – *please*!' he said, thrusting something into her hands. Then he turned and dashed away to be swallowed up in the crowd.

Ginny glanced at the folded piece of paper in her hands and then across at Donny. 'Better read it,' he advised solemnly. She unfolded the paper and read the handwritten message.

> *If you want to see the REAL Cormac come to the stables tonight after 8 o'clock. But don't tell anyone. I'll be there and I have something very IMPORTANT to tell you. Cormac is really fine. You'll see that for yourself. Please come. Martin.*

'Does it mean we won't be having our dinner together tonight?' asked Donny dejectedly.

Ginny nodded. 'I'm afraid so, Donny.' She had already made up her mind what she must do.

Seven

He was waiting for her on the opposite side of the road from the dirt track leading to Cafferkey's stables. Ginny, cycling along with the casual air of someone just out for an evening spin, had guessed he might want to intercept her on arrival. She knew it wouldn't be sensible to ride up to Mr Cafferkey's front door and simply ask to speak to Martin.

Nervousness mingled with relief in his manner as he greeted her. 'I can't stay long,' she pointed out firmly. 'I shouldn't be here as it is.'

When he promised that she needn't stay a minute longer than she wanted to, she added that all she wanted was to clear up the mystery of Cormac's alleged injury and his extraordinary performance on the racecourse.

'It'll be no mystery in a few minutes. I'll be telling you the lot. So will you come up to the yard now?'

Soon Ginny was enjoying the sense of taking command of the situation, the complete reversal of the role she'd played at their first meeting on the wooded slope that now seemed to tower above them. Although Martin suggested it would be a good idea to leave her bike concealed under the hedge he had no reservations about her approaching the house openly on foot with him. Cafferkey, he explained, had gone out for the evening to celebrate and was unlikely to be home before midnight at the earliest. He had taken Jackie, his stable-girl, with him and so Martin was in sole charge of the establishment.

'What does he have to celebrate?' Ginny asked. 'I should have thought he'd be down in the dumps with Cormac losing.'

Martin allowed himself a bit of a laugh. 'But the guv'nor knew our horse couldn't win. So Light-keeper was the only horse capable of winning. So the money went on Lightkeeper, piles of it. It's been his best trick for years. He has the money now to pay all his debts, or most of 'em, unless he's a fool and throws it all away again on the booze.'

'But why were you so positive Cormac *couldn't* win? I mean, lots of people round here had heard the rumour that Cormac is a pretty good horse. If he'd been ridden properly he probably *would* have won. Surely it's better to win money on your own horse than risk it on somebody else's?'

'I'll show you why.' They entered the stable block and Martin walked over to a loose box that backed on to the house; it was, Ginny recognized, the box from which the stable girl had taken the grey horse while she herself had watched through binoculars from the hillside. 'Come in,' Martin invited her, 'and meet the real Cormac.'

The moment she stepped into the box she had no doubt at all that this was the horse she'd seen in the stream. Momentarily his ears twitched back but immediately pricked up again. She reached up to fondle them and quickly located the tiny nick that totally confirmed identification. His untroubled eyes studied her with interest and Ginny had the feeling that he was trying to remember where it was they'd met previously!

Martin was trying to show her something. Bending low, he cupped his hand behind the grey's knee on his near fore. 'Can ye see it?' he wanted to know. 'Almost gone now, it has, but still a slight puffiness. But in a day or two the old fella will be as sound as a drum again.'

Ginny had to peer hard to detect anything out of the ordinary. In any case, she didn't need to see the place where the tendon had been inflamed: she had known for some time what had been wrong with Cormac.

'You saw him in the stream, didn't you?' Martin was saying. 'I guessed that when Carmen told me the English girl had been making inquiries in the village. You must have seen him just before we took him out of the water. Normally, there's not a soul goes up there on the moorland.'

'It was cruel, terribly cruel,' Ginny said scathingly. 'Inhuman. You'd just no cause to do anything as bad as that.'

'Ah, but it wasn't, don't ye see? Cormac now, he's an intelligent fella, he *knew* the running water was doing him the world of good. Cold water, running against the leg, well, it's a wonderful cure. The trick worked, too. But not fast enough, that was the difficulty.' Martin fumbled in his pocket and found a titbit for the horse; all the time he talked he was stroking Cormac's neck with genuine affection. 'Well, come on now,' he said, turning to Ginny. 'I'll show you the switch horse.'

'The *switch* horse?'

But Martin, after giving Cormac a farewell pat and then securing his door, made no reply before conducting Ginny across the yard and into another box. As soon as she saw the occupant she gasped. She couldn't help it. The dappled grey she was looking at was Cormac's double. The likeness was absolutely uncanny.

'Amazing, isn't it?' Martin remarked almost gleefully. 'We could hardly believe it ourselves when we saw the two together, side by side. To tell the truth, even Cormac himself was a bit – startled. Must have thought we'd found his long lost twin brother for him! Might be that, too, for all we know.'

'What's his name?' she asked. When she tried to stroke him the grey backed away, trembling a little; he was still restless after his exertions of the afternoon. His temperament was quite different from Cormac's, she realized.

'Ry-Tansa!' Martin spelt it out, letter by letter. 'Means Right Answer, you see. Good, that, isn't it? Jackie it was that found him, so she named him. As the guv'nor said, it was the right answer for us all right. First joke I've ever heard him make, really.'

'But, Martin, why did you run him in place of Cormac? I mean, if Cormac wasn't fit you could just have taken him out of the race. It wouldn't have mattered, you could have run him in another race later on. Why did you have to be so – so deceitful?'

Martin's smile faded, but he still looked quite pleased with himself. 'Ah, things are never as simple as they sometimes seem. We all knew Cormac was a good horse, a *really* good horse, best we've ever had, I'm thinking. The bumper race at the Junction was going to be just the right race for him, win easy he would. The guv'nor would make a packet out of it – with his bets, I mean. Only one danger: Lightkeeper. And then Cormac goes and gets this strained tendon, a pretty bad one. Now, if Cormac didn't run, Lightkeeper would be no price at all. You'd need to put a house on him to win a few bricks, if you follow me.'

He paused but, when there was no response, continued: 'So, if we put it about that Cormac was a dark horse with a bit of a chance, well then, Lightkeeper would stay a decent price. If we let Ry-Tansa run in his place, with no one knowing the difference, then the guv'nor could make his money. We put Ry-Tansa through his paces. Not a bad little horse at all but not in Cormac's class. So, as the guv'nor said, we couldn't lose – just so long as Lightkeeper didn't do anything mad like fall and break a leg. Now, wasn't it lovely the way it all worked out as Cafferkey said it would?'

'But every racehorse has a passport and it's got to be examined when the horse arrives at the racecourse stables,' Ginny said. 'I learned all about that when I went with Tamela to Pershore. So how did you manage to persuade them at Killwaylow that

Ry-Tansa was actually Cormac? Did you – did you *bribe* the attendant?'

'No need for that,' was the cheerful answer. 'Passports aren't all that important unless they're checked very carefully. But, usually, that only happens the first time the horse runs – and Cormac had already run once. Anyway, the officials at the Junction know our stable pretty well. They wouldn't suspect us of anything. Strangers are the ones they worry about.'

There was one other matter that was puzzling Ginny. 'Why are you telling *me* all this? There's nothing to stop me going off to tell the racecourse authorities, the police, anyone.'

With a very gentle and sweeping motion Martin was running his hand along the grey's flank. Ry-Tansa seemed as calm now as the stable-lad. 'Well now, I'm thinking you're a smart girl, Ginny. I think you'd just about worked it out for yourself because you'd seen the two horses. Nobody else outside the stable's done that. It's still a secret everywhere else. I thought if I told you then you'd be willing to help me.'

'*Help* you? But how?

'Get me a job in a racing stable in England, one where they'll give me a chance to ride. That's all.'

The idea was so startling that Ginny hardly knew

how to answer. All she could think of was what a nerve he'd got to ask such a thing. 'But I can't do that,' she said eventually. 'I only know one trainer, Mr McDade, and he isn't looking for any more stable-lads at present. Anyway, after what you've just told me I don't think I –'

'But it's the contact I need,' Martin cut in eagerly. 'Trainers are always recommending lads and jockeys to one another – that's the way it goes in racing. You could fix it through McDade so I could get a trial. Sure and I'd prove in no time that I can be a top rider.'

'After what your stable's been fixing with Cormac. . . .'

'Ah, forget all that, Ginny! No harm's been done. A few punters lost their money on him. That sort of thing happens all the time with any non-trier. So it's not important. We're only a little stable, we haven't had a winner for a year and we need winners to keep going. If Cormac had stayed fit we'd have had that winner. When you're unlucky like that, well you have to make your own luck. It was my luck, I'm thinking, when I met you. Because, Ginny, you're the only person who can help me. I've no contacts of my own in England. So, *please*!'

'I'll, er, I'll have to think about it,' replied Ginny, playing for time. 'Listen, Martin, I want to know what's going to happen to Ry-Tansa in future. Because if –'

'Ah, I know what you're thinking, Ginny. But forget it. That's a trick we can't pull off twice. Something as complicated as that will only work once. Anyway, Cormac will be as fit as a fiddle and ready to run for his life in his next race. Sure, an' he'll win it like a dream!'

'Yes, I expect he will. But I asked about Ry-Tansa: what's going to happen to him?'

'Well now, he'll be disposed of, won't he? Have to be, you see. So –'

'*Disposed of?*' Ginny was horrified. Immediately she imagined the grey being removed to a hiding place, a gun being put to his head, and then . . .

At that moment they heard someone calling. 'Mart'n. MART'N! Where the devil are you?'

Martin's hand shot up to his face, instantly paler than the colour of Ry-Tansa's coat. 'Oh, glory, that's Cafferkey, back early,' he whispered, scrubbing finger-nails across his teeth. 'You'll have to get out, fast as you can. He mustn't know you've been here.'

Ginny was just as alarmed as he was, though for different reasons. But, as Martin was darting out of the box, she grabbed his arm. 'Listen, if you want my help then you've got to help me – to save Ry-Tansa. If anything bad happens to him

110

I'll – I'll make sure everyone knows about the switch.'

'All right, all right! But I've got to go now, otherwise . . .'

She wasn't able to detain him any longer. 'I'll get in touch, tomorrow if possible. But remember, Martin – this horse mustn't be harmed!' He nodded that he understood – and fled.

Moments later she peered round the stable-door, praying that the yard would be clear. It was. Martin had been summoned into the house and, thankfully, he and Cafferkey were still in there. Ginny murmured a farewell to Ry-Tansa, with a promise to see him again soon, and then raced out to the gate that led into the paddock. Afterwards she could never recall how she clambered over it, only that every second of her escape she was expecting Cafferkey to appear and bellow at her to stop.

She was among the screening trees on the hill above the house before she dared to pause to get her breath back. Then, very slowly, and by the longest route, she made her way to the main road.

On the long ride to Ballytor Ginny thought of nothing else but the plight of Ry-Tansa. How she was going to save him she had no idea. One thing, though, was certain: unless she thought of something quickly, the grey horse was doomed.

Eight

When, two days later, Ginny set out again for Cafferkey's racing stables it was in the front seat of a
hire car. In the back were her mother and Mrs
Nancy Anderson, the leading lady in Corwick
Amateur Dramatic Society's most recent production. As experienced actresses about to take part
in another performance, albeit a distinctly unusual
one, they were managing to keep their personal
feelings largely under control. Ginny's emotions
were thoroughly mixed: excited, apprehensive, im-
patient, determined, joyful. Each mood seemed to
take hold of her in turn.

The driver glanced across at her with a very
friendly grin. 'You'll be a very happy young lady
when this little journey is over, I shouldn't
wonder,' he remarked.

'Oh, I hope so, Mr Mailey.' Ginny squeezed her

shoulders inwards in anticipatory pleasure. 'Heavens, yes! I've just got to hope that everything turns our all right.'

'Everything's going to be fine, honey, just fine,' Mrs Anderson promised in a pronounced American drawl. 'So just relax, honey.'

Ginny gave her a smile of gratitude and managed not to laugh as she added: 'Thanks Aunt Nancy.'

For the next few miles she did as she was told, easing herself into the contours of the seat and reflecting on the events of the past forty-eight hours. To say the least, they'd contained a few surprises. On her return to Ballytor after her escape from Cafferkey's, she had continued to ponder the problem of how she was going to rescue Ry-Tansa. By the following morning she'd concocted several plans, but as soon as she started to work out the details, she was forced to concede that none of them was remotely feasible.

Ginny would have liked to try and discuss the matter with her mother, but that was out of the question for the present. It was not only the last day of the Drama Festival, but the one on which the Corwick Society were giving their performance; and the results were being announced at a ceremony in the evening. So Jane Luellen was too keyed-up to do anything but concentrate on her part in the play.

In the end she realized there was only one person whose aid she could enlist: Donal McCormick. So she'd gone to see him and poured out the whole story from the moment she'd first seen the real Cormac. To her surprise, *he* didn't seem a bit surprised by any of it. He had guessed from her mood just before and during the last race at the Junction that something serious was bothering her. Ever since horse-racing began, he added, various characters had perpetrated various crafty little fiddles: sometimes they'd got away with them, sometimes they'd been caught in the act. The really cunning feature of Cafferkey's deception was that it couldn't be *proved*, even if the two horses were now to be seen standing side by side: suspicion alone wasn't enough in these circumstances. The dangerous moment for Cafferkey, the one when his runner's passport was examined, had passed. Unless he was stupid enough to attempt that trick again he had got away with it.

But, Ginny wanted to know, how was the trainer going to 'dispose of' Ry-Tansa? Ah! exclaimed Donny, that was an easy question: he would sell the horse. 'Cafferkey doesn't only train horses, he deals in 'em. A low-class dealer he may be, but a dealer for all that!' Ginny persisted: but who would buy him? 'Well now,' said Donny to her utter amazement, 'I might. Now, don't look at me

114

like that, Ginny! I've owned one or two horses in my time and I was thinking yesterday it would be great fun to have another. Seemed to me that your Cormac – sorry, Ry-Tansa – has a lot of potential. He could make up into a very decent chaser one day. Looks really strong.'

After getting an assurance that he wasn't contemplating buying the horse just for her sake, Ginny delightedly joined in plotting how the purchase could be made. Because he and Cafferkey were acquainted with one another Donny couldn't do the buying himself. In any case, the trainer would try to ensure that he sold to someone who would take the horse to live a long way from Skelhouley. 'What we need,' mused Donny, 'is someone to *pose* as a likely buyer – perhaps a rich American widow who's fallen in love with the idea of owning a grey horse. Cafferkey would fall for that, wouldn't be able to resist the lure of all those lovely dollars!'

It was then that Ginny had an inspiration: 'Mum could do it! She *is* an actress, practically as good as a professional. Hey, how about that for quick thinking?' Donny was quite taken with that suggestion, but as their scheme evolved, it was clear that it needed strengthening in one or two places. Eventually it was decided that it should be Ginny who coveted the grey horse; and the rich American would be her aunt. To make the story even more convincing Ginny's mother could be present as herself and cast some doubt on whether the horse really was quite suitable for her daughter to ride in point-to-point races in England. 'That,' grinned Ginny, 'should be an easy role for her to play!'

As resourceful as ever, Donny had arranged for a friend to make a phone-call to Cafferkey to confirm that the trainer had a grey horse for sale. He ensured that funds would be available, some of them in dollars, for the purchase; laid on a hire car and transport for the horse; and alerted one of his former trainers with the news that he was thinking of becoming a racehorse owner again and that the animal would arrive at the trainer's yard in a day or so.

All they needed then was the support of Mrs Luellen and another member of the Dramatic Society. Donny had his fingers crossed, but he had no need to worry: his luck was still in. Because, that evening, the Society's production of *Don't look at me like that!* was awarded second prize in the Festival. Along with the rest of the cast, Jane Luellen was overjoyed – and in the mood to agree to almost anything. It was actually she who suggested that Mrs Anderson should be asked to play the part of the rich American widow. 'Oh yes, indeed, I love real-life drama,' enthused the leading lady. 'Why, that role will suit me just beautifully!'

Now, as the hire car cruised through Skelhouley on the way to the last act, Nancy Anderson was diligently playing her part to the full. If this horse was the one that Ginny wanted then she was to have it: it would be the *perfect* gift after they'd all enjoyed such a wonderful, *wonderful* holiday in Ireland, dear, dear old Ireland.

Dutifully, Jane Luellen raised mild doubts. A horse would cost a terrible amount of money; it would cost a terrible amount to feed it and keep it; it might be far too powerful for Ginny to ride....

Mr Mailey leaned across to Ginny. 'Who do you think will win the argument?'

'Oh, my aunt, I expect. She usually does. She always gets her own way at home with my uncle.'

'I can believe that!' murmured Mr Mailey, stifling a laugh.

The car turned into the dirt track that led to Cafferkey's. Suddenly, Ginny's nervousness returned in full measure. She was praying that Martin would keep his promise to stay out of sight today. Earlier, telephoning in the guise of a girl friend, she had warned him about the visit, giving her own promise that if all went well she would ask Mr McDade to find him a job in an English racing stable.

All seemed well for, as the car came to a halt in the yard, there was only one person in sight: slightly built, bow-legged and leaning his back against the gate into the paddock: Cafferkey himself. He had, Ginny decided, a rather ferrety look about him, though he was grinning a welcome.

'Ah, Mr Cafferkey, it's a real pleasure to meet you,' said Mrs Anderson, striding across to grasp his hand. She waved her free hand vaguely in the direction of 'my sister and my niece from England' without attempting to introduce them properly. Then, briskly, she continued: 'Now, we don't have much time, unfortunately. Lot of miles still to go, lot of horses maybe still to see. Time, you know, Mr Cafferkey, is money where I come from in New York City. Certainly is! Now...'

Such speed was not at all what Cafferkey had bargained for: he was used to doing business in a leisurely way. Already the torrent of words was overwhelming him.

'Jackie!' he bawled, recovering a little of his authority. 'Just bring the little fella out, will you now.' It hadn't been lost on him that the American lady had lined up other prospective purchases.

The stable door swung open and Jackie emerged, leading Ry-Tansa, already saddled. Ginny caught her breath: the grey horse, perfectly groomed, looked beautiful. She moved across to stroke his

118

neck and then fondle his ears. Ry-Tansa rolled away from her touch, but not before she had assured herself that the ears were unmarked. Involuntarily, Ginny glanced towards Cormac's box but, as she'd guessed, it was empty; probably Martin was out with him at this moment, miles away from the risk of an accidental encounter.

'Well, honey, what do you think of him?' Mrs Anderson was inquiring forcefully.

'Oh, he's just lovely, Aunt Nancy,' Ginny responded truthfully. 'He's just, well, what I want. Perfect.'

'Ginny, I do think he's rather – rather big,' Jane Luellen put in doubtfully. 'I rather think he may be, well, too powerful for you.'

'Nonsense, Jane! She's a strong girl, *and* still growing. Jane, you can't keep her in cotton wool for ever. Honey, let's see you sit that horse.'

Ginny, who'd been having difficulty in smothering a grin after seeing the look on her mother's face, thankfully accepted a leg-up from Jackie.

'Why, honey, you look an absolute picture up there – doesn't she, Mr Cafferkey?'

The trainer eagerly nodded his agreement; he could hardly do otherwise. Almost instantly, however, his contentment with the way things were going was eroded. For, having asked the price of the horse, and been told what it was, Mrs Anderson

promptly repeated one of her favourite words:
'Nonsense! Far too high, Mr Cafferkey, far too
high!' Then she quoted the price *she* had in mind
– which happened to be exactly half of his.

'Ah, now, ma'am, I'll be bankrupting meself if
I even listen to such talk,' he tried to tell her.

'Mr Cafferkey, I'm not here to have a hassle. I
know the value of things. I *know* what I'll pay.' Then,
opening her capacious handbag, she appeared
to search for something. 'Darn it, I was sure I had
some smokes,' she added in an exasperated
tone. In order to dig deeper she had first to
remove something from the bag: an exceedingly
thick roll of American dollars. As she displayed it,
Cafferkey's eyes fastened moistly on that tempting
prize. Almost in a whisper, he dropped his price
by a couple of hundred. Mrs Anderson, glancing
up, retorted: 'I'll go another fifty – and not a cent
more. Now that's my last word, Mr Cafferkey.'

At that moment they all heard the sounds of a
heavy vehicle grinding up the track towards them.
'What's that?' Cafferkey asked worriedly.

'My horse-box,' replied Mrs Anderson matter-
of-factly. 'I said we had no time to waste. So the
box follows me till I've bought a horse. Then, the
moment we have the animal's travel documents, off
he goes to England. But I guess you and I are not
going to do business after all, Mr Cafferkey. Pity.

122

Ginny, darling, slip down and tell the driver to head for our next scheduled stop.'

Obediently, Ginny slid to the ground just as the van shuddered to a halt outside the yard.

'Wait now!' Cafferkey cried. It was that remark about the horse's instant departure over the sea that clinched the deal for him. He capitulated. 'The horse is yours, ma'am, at your price. It's a rare bargain you'll be getting at that.'

'Very handsome of you, Mr Cafferkey,' said Mrs Anderson with a gracious smile and a firm handshake. Then, while Ginny supervised the loading of Ry-Tansa into the horse-box, buyer and seller went into a huddle to complete the financial arrangements. Mrs Anderson handed over a substantial portion of the purchase price and it was agreed that the remainder would be paid when the horse had passed a veterinary examination.

After more handshaking all round, it was time to go. 'Untold pleasure, that's what you'll be getting from that fine horse,' was Cafferkey's parting comment to Ginny. 'I hate to think I'll never be seeing him again.'

'Well, you never know, Mr Cafferkey,' she responded lightly. 'Maybe, one day, you will.'

At that moment Ginny rather wished she could tell the trainer that he certainly *would* see the horse again. For it was part of Donny's plan to run

Ry-Tansa locally, if possible at the same meeting and on the same day that Cormac was running.

Plenty of eyebrows would be raised at the sight of identical greys – and they'd shoot still higher when Donny allowed it to be known that Ry-Tansa had been bought out of Cafferkey's stable. That fact alone would act as a public warning to Cafferkey never again to attempt a 'switch horse' trick.

As soon as they were back in Ballytor and the hire car had driven away Ginny flung her arms round Mrs Anderson in gratitude for all she'd done.

'No need to thank me, dear,' said her 'American aunt', beaming. 'I enjoyed every minute of that little drama. Frankly, it was one of the best parts I've had for years!'

That evening at the Junction Hotel, Killwaylow, there was a celebration dinner. The host was Donal McCormick and his guests were Nancy Anderson, Jane Luellen and Ginny. The food was excellent, the champagne even better than excellent, but, towards the end of the meal, sadness seemed to creep into Donny's eyes.

'Why, Mr McCormick, whatever's wrong?' Mrs Anderson inquired in rising alarm.

'Oh, I was just thinking that tomorrow you'll all

be back in England – and maybe I'll never be seeing you again.'

'Nonsense!' Mrs Anderson snorted. 'Of course you will. We're coming back to Ballytor next year to *win* the Festival!'

'And I'm coming back to see Ry-Tansa win for his new owner,' Ginny promised.

'Ah,' said Donny with a contented smile, 'that's just what I was hoping you'd be saying.'

Then, like successful conspirators, he and Ginny exchanged calculated winks.

Also by Michael Hardcastle

Motocross Stories

Fast From the Gate
The Green Machine
Roar to Victory
Tiger of the Track

Football Stories

Away From Home
Free Kick
Half a Team
Mascot
Soccer Special
The Team That Wouldn't Give In
United

Riding Stories

The Saturday Horse
Winning Rider

Caught Out   (A Cricket Story)
Rival Games   (An Athletics Story)
The Shooters   (A Netball Story

THE SATURDAY HORSE

Michael Hardcastle

When Ginny first sees the beautiful chestnut
racehorse she is determined to become accepted at
the stables and look after him. The owners feel
Tamela will never be a winner but Ginny's faith in
him is unshaken. If only she can find out what the
matter is . . .

A fascinating story of life in a racing stable, full of
drama both on and off the racecourse.

WINNING RIDER

Michael Hardcastle

Rachel's burning ambition is to ride Catch Boy, the five-year-old hurdler, against professional jockeys. But Catch Boy's trainer thinks he's a loser, a non-starter. How can Rachel convince him that he's wrong, that Catch Boy is a winner – and that she is the rider to prove it?

A dramatic story with all the tension and excitement of the track.

By Mary O'Hara

Three gripping stories, featuring the McLaughlin
family and the horses of the Goose Bar Ranch, set
against the powerful background of the Wyoming
countryside.

My Friend Flicka
Thunderhead
Green Grass of Wyoming

A Selected List of Fiction from Mammoth

The prices shown below were correct at the time of going to press.